An Unthinkable Crime. An Unlikely Redemption.

# NUBBY

An Unthinkable Crime. An Unlikely Redemption.

# NUBBY

## NANCY PAUL

NUBBY
An Unthinkable Crime. An Unlikely Redemption.
By Nancy Paul

Nancy Paul
Indianapolis
317-755-0434
desprithousewife.com
nancyschmollpaul@gmail.com

ISBN: 978-0-9894388-0-3

Library of Congress Control Number: 2013907049

Cover and interior design: Suzanne Parada
Editor: Janet Schwind
Photography: Steve Polston
Author Photography: Ian Smith

## DEDICATIONS

To God, thank you for *not* being a gentleman.

To my family—biological, adoptive, spiritual—who've each of us stood at the edge of our own cliffs and there found it: relief, redemption, hope and healing.

To Heather and Billy who went before us, to warn everyone, I presume. I love and miss you every day.

## ACKNOWLEDGEMENTS

My husband supported this book completely by carving out time for me to disappear and write, listening to my ideas and first draft from cover to cover, and allowing it to become part of the family. "Good morning, Nance. Good morning, Nubby."

My kids gave me tons of feedback about where the story should go. The characters became real to them and when I translated some of their ideas to print, they became more real to me, too. At the end of the project, they worked ahead on their homeschool lessons to give me an entire week to finish the last few chapters (um, also so they could play video games).

Janet Schwind helped me at every level of the creative and production process. She encouraged, edited, brainstormed, encouraged some more, told a joke or two, which made me laugh, which was nice. Her professional experience and raw talent were instrumental in helping me know what to do and how to do it and stuff like that.

Marcia Calhoun got sucked into the story despite the fact that she hates reading things chapter by chapter. She gave me feedback as a reader, what worked, what didn't, what she liked, what she didn't. I obsessed about this book and she let me—over sushi, over Facebook, over the phone. She was my literary cheerleader, asking for more Nubby. So I kept writing.

My church is full of super creative people, which makes sense to me since we have the Creator of the entire universe as our head. The Indy Vineyard and IVAC group let me bounce ideas off of and share my talents with them. They gave me permission and encouragement to pursue dreams.

My Celebrate Recovery group at Mt. Comfort Vineyard saw a transformation in my personal life over the few months I wrote this book. In the beginning I was still locked in bondage to grief, depression and anxiety. Because of their loving acceptance, my perseverance in working the twelve steps and God's grace, I not only became free to feel the positive emotions as deeply as I'd felt the negative, but also free to have fun and create again.

# CONTENTS

# PART ONE

# DARKNESS

# The Birthday

She rode the ups and downs of this, her first labor and delivery, like a long-awaited roller coaster. She'd begun the day curious, anxious, ignorantly confident. Now there was only terror. Seismic shocks ripped through her body and morphed into screams as they exited. These echoed through the hospital corridor, ignored by staff who were attending to others. Her own doctor and nurse stood calmly, professionally at the other end of her legs, coaching and coaxing. She white-knuckled the bed's rails as she concentrated on hearing and doing what they instructed. "Push," she bore down forcefully on her uterine muscles. "Breath," she sucked air through her clenched teeth. "Rest," she lay back and waited for the next wave of agony.

"You're doing great, honey. You're going to be okay." The nurse's gentle, motherly tone infuriated her. *I'm not a child,* she thought vehemently. Exhaustion muted her.

She closed her glare behind swollen, puffy eyelids and let herself sink back into the mattress. So soft. Clean smelling white blankets enveloped her, inviting her to sleep. Her muscles relaxed and she drifted. They had been kind to her here, speaking in hushed, even tones, turning her pillows over to cool the hot skin of her face. She felt warm and comfortable. Safe.

SLAP! She felt her mother's words like a hand across her cheek, "You 'member this, girlie. Kindness is jest the tool they use to find yer weakness." Sitting up, she grunted, "Fuck you!" and began to ride the next contraction. She would not be weak.

Anger fueled and channeled her remaining energy. A movie reel played in her head, each image a cog in the mechanical lift deliberately elevating her mind and emotions—steeling herself for one last wild loop on this crazy ride. Mother standing over her with "The Fear" hidden behind her back. Pills in blues and whites that make you grow taller. Teacher telling her to stay after school so he could give her "extra credit." Pills in reds and yellows that make you grow shorter.

She wanted pills now, but Mother wasn't here to give her the right ones. She would not be weak.

She felt it full force then. This time the scream had no breath. It jumped back down her throat and through her body, wrapped itself tightly around the thing inside her, riding the contractions out. It was kicking, clawing, grasping and ripping at her internal organs—she could feel it. Hot, sticky blood soaked her thighs; there was a flurry of panicked activity. "Too much blood," she heard the shouts of the medical staff as a whisper. The pain was screaming at her, "YOU BAD GIRLIE! YOU GONNA GIT IT NOW! I'M GONNA PUT THE FEAR IN YOU!"

She gave one last push, scrunching her eyes tightly to block out the sounds, heard and felt the tearing down below, like a piece of paper being torn in two. Like teacher's paper. "Not good enough, Girlie. You gonna have to stay after school so's I kin give you 'extra credit.'"

She felt it coming out of her. It gushed liquids, squeezed razor blades and plopped a mass of tissue onto the cold, wet gurney. Her last two thoughts before passing out were the realization that the roller coaster voices were all the same—the voice of Mother—and that she must have finally pushed 'the fear' out, because she didn't feel it anymore. From that point on she felt nothing.

## CHAPTER ONE

# The Problem

"Ma'am, it's time." Without looking up from the novel in her lap, she held up a finger to motion that she'd be a minute. She finished the last page of the book, closed it and glanced up to see the doctor pulling a new white sheet up over the girl's head before leaving the room. The hefty woman stood up, the chair screeching across the floor. She placed the paperback onto the seat, finished with it, then hoisted her worn brown paisley carpet bag off the floor before stepping over to the waiting nurse, who smiled and held the bundle in her arms toward her.

"Isn't she just beaut—?"

"Yes, fine, then. A girl. I'll take it from here."

"But there's something you should know."

"I have done this many times before. I am quite capable of far more, thank you very much." The terse reply worked to harden the nurse's face.

"Alright, it's just that she—"

"I said I will take it from here." The woman held out her hands to take the baby. The exasperated nurse placed her in the woman's arms and turned indignantly to exit.

"Nurse!"

She turned warily.

"I assume you have shredded the documentation?"

"Of course. I followed procedure as usual."

"Excellent. That is as it should be. You and the doctor are both very well compensated, as you know. That is all. You are dismissed."

The nurse left, frowning.

This new bundle the hefty woman shoved quickly into her large bag before exiting smartly out the door. As it closed, a sudden burst of wind ruffled the pages of the book she'd abandoned. "Extra Large Print" was stamped across the front of a steamy scene of a man and woman locked in embrace.

She marched to the side exit where a black sedan waited for her. Her driver stood silently watching her, just as he'd silently watched countless young women over the past seven years enter the building with a company representative by their side. Some of the girls were obviously with child, bellies protruding out the bottoms of their t-shirts, over the waistbands of their jeans. Their escort, a slender woman dressed nicely with her hair swept up in a loose bun, smiled and chattered as she confidently led them into the building. He could hear snippets of their conversation, "You'll love it here. There are lots of girls just like you who've found help. You and your baby are in good hands." The strange thing was he'd never once seen a girl leave. But he had figured out how the babies were transported out. It was in a new black Rolls Royce sedan containing a spineless man in a chauffer's hat and a crazy woman with a bag.

"Evening, ma'am," her driver held the back door open without mention of her package. He'd learned not to, and he'd learned this the way the hardest and most remembered lessons are taught—through pain. He feared her tongue lashing, he feared her icy glare, he feared her manipulation and control. Mostly he feared another visit to the dark back room in the warehouse. His paychecks were the only thing that helped him stomach her very presence. So he kept to the script, remembering to avoid looking at the thing she'd wrapped haphazardly in an old, careworn blanket, and stuffed carelessly into her ratty old bag, remembering not to make eye contact, and once again convinced himself it was just a job. Wasn't any sense in thinking much about it anyway. He wasn't paid to think, just drive.

"Dickerson. We will be taking our usual route tonight."

"Yes, ma'am," he said, thinking that there was nothing usual about the route or what they were doing out on a night like this in the first place, but there wasn't any sense in thinking about any of that either. He watched her toss her bag into the back seat before hefting her large frame in next to it. Fumbling with the seat belt, as she always did, she moved out of the way for him to lean in and click it into place. He glanced over, wondering at the contents of the bag. Where did they go, what did they do with them?

"Excuse me, is there a problem Dickerson?"

"Nothin', ma'am. I got it. No problems."

"Good. Now will you be sitting back here or driving? Because I am fairly certain you are paid to drive. Not think, not interfere."

"Yes ma'am, I mean, no ma'am. Uh, let me get your door for you, ma'am."

She reached down to check on her bag. Satisfied, she knocked on the frosted glass and Dickerson drove away.

He drove a few blocks to get onto the highway, then east to the outer belt. Tonight would be counterclockwise. It was Monday, after all. He had triple checked—his watch, his phone, the little planner with the red X's for west and the blue X's for east—his threefold insurance that he'd never mess up the route again. His employers were very specific and detailed. They were also very intolerant of even the most minor mistakes.

He drove to the darkly lit building exactly halfway across town and put the black Rolls Royce into park. She wordlessly left the car and walked toward the door, bag heavily slanting backward. She paused to adjust and balance its weight, then entered the store.

He hated that bag because of what was in it. It disgusted him that she so casually carried it around with her, but he was also equally relieved that she didn't leave it in the car alone with him. What would he do if it whimpered or cried? Would he try to comfort it? Seemed like that'd be the right thing to do, but he'd learned long ago that right feels wrong and wrong feels right. Seemed wrong to let it cry though.

Truth was, they never did cry. He'd not heard so much as a hiccup outta that backseat in all the years he'd been driving "Miss Crazy," as he called her in his head. He never said this out loud, not even when he was alone. Never. Seemed risky enough to think it. Chiding himself for concerning himself with things that he shouldn't, he turned on a jazz station and waited.

She came out with another thick paperback in hand, stepped into the car and rapped on the glass. Dickerson turned off the radio so that he could give all his attention to driving, then completed the route. North past the cookie-cutter housing developments that took advantage of the outer belt's suburban provisions. Past the commercial and industrial areas he weaved an indirect route to their destination in the inner city. Down a dark parking ramp whose gate opened only after he placed his thumb into the reader. Further still into the lowest level, and then through a wall that opened only for Miss Crazy's meaty thumbprint. He parked and opened the door for her. He let her gather her things by herself, having learned that offering to help her would be seen as an insult.

He watched her enter the big red door he'd never seen the other side of, then he turned to exit to the stairwell for the security escort to the next level up where his own car waited. He was done for the night and breathed a sigh of relief. He'd made no mistakes, at least no glaring ones, so he knew he'd be called to return tomorrow.

"Hi, Dickerson." The older man was greeted by the young guard striding over to him.

"Hello, Frank." The two men walked up the stairs in silence, knowing any conversation beyond this greeting was forbidden. The differences between the two men were almost comical as they walked side by side. Frank's tall, muscular build filled out his dark blue security uniform while Dickerson's short, round body threatened to squeeze out of the buttons of his chauffer jacket. "Good night, Frank."

"G'night, Dickerson." Frank gave him a little wave before returning to his post.

Dickerson unlocked his green Mercury Sable and slid into the front seat. He started the ignition, the sound of Coltrane's sax filling his ears. As he backed out and began his drive up through the basement of this secure complex back into the real world outside, his anxiety began to wane. Leaving the dim parking garage he pushed up the volume, pulled off his hat and loosened his tie. His trip time took about twenty minutes at night, when there was no traffic. Longer, of course, in the morning when everyone was rushing into the city to do important things for important people. In the morning he was glad for this longer drive, as he spent the time mentally rehearsing his route, his scripted responses, his every action. It was almost like the commute in was a time for him to pump himself up into a state of ready anxiety for the expectations they had for him, and the commute home was where he deflated again, breathed again, became himself again.

⌇

He reached over to grab a piece of Dentyne from his glove box, yet another part of his evening ritual, and suddenly felt his phone vibrate in his pocket. Startled, he immediately began to turn the car around as he answered. "Yes, ma'am?" He knew who it was without looking at the phone. There were only two people who had this number—the one who'd given him the phone in the first place, who he'd never seen since, and Miss Crazy.

"You need to return immediately, Dickerson."

"Yes, ma'am." He hung up, fished for his hat in the darkness of the passenger seat where he'd casually thrown it, and concentrated on breathing again. This had never happened before. He tried to tighten his tie but realized he could not do so with only one hand. He resolved to take care of that important detail upon his arrival, drove quickly back to the ramp and into the deeper garage. He hurried to Frank's security post, smoothing his uniform with nervous, sweaty hands.

"What's going on, Frank?"

"I don't know. I guess there's a problem."

Frank took him all the way to the big red door. He opened it with a key that looked unlike anything Dickerson had ever seen before. It was a small, red plastic oval, which Frank placed against the keyhole, then activated some sort of laser light with his forefinger. The lock mechanism inside beeped and clicked open. He motioned for Dickerson to go in first, searched the area outside the door warily, then followed him in. "Keep your gloves on. Go to the elevator and then to the top floor. They're waiting for you."

Anxiety threatened to take his knees out from under him, but he took a deep breath and began walking. The top floor happened to be the fiftieth. He'd had no idea how many levels the building had, as the design of its exterior gave no clues. As the elevator doors opened on a spacious, elegantly decorated hallway, Dickerson wondered for the millionth time who exactly he worked for.

He'd gotten this job as a fluke seven years before. He was working valet at one of the restaurants downtown on the circle. A man drove up slowly in a silver Bentley, rolled down his tinted window and a strong, musky sweet smell wafted out of the interior. He spoke directly to Dickerson, "Can you drive a car this nice, redneck?" He'd laughed, thinking the man had been joking. "I said, can you?"

"Uh, yes, sir."

"Can you park it on the top of the valet garage, on the south end?"

"Yes sir, no problem." Dickerson's experience taught him that tips were typically increased in proportion to how many ridiculous requests were carried out and personal jabs accepted.

"And I will pay you one-thousand dollars to leave it in neutral."

"Well, sir, that's an incline there and it will probably roll right..."

"Let me talk to another valet then, since you are incapable of such a simple request and obviously don't like money."

"Oh, no, sir, I like money. I can do it, no questions asked. Sorry sir. I'll do it."

"And then you'll forget this conversation?"

"What conversation?" Dickerson smiled. The man nodded, shoved a stack of hundreds and a key into his hand, then abruptly walked away down the sidewalk.

Dickerson pocketed the money and did what the man asked. It was a no-brainer when he visualized the hefty bill from the hospital lying on his kitchen counter at home. This tip would certainly put a dent in it.

He was fired later that night when the car rolled backward down the slight incline of the valet garage, picked up speed before busting through the flimsy guardrail and landed—a crumpled mess of glass and metal—into a dumpster behind Shimpy's Restaurant.

Dickerson was three beers into the process of forgetting that he was now unemployed when someone sat down next to him. A familiar voice asked, "You want to be a driver for me?"

"Yes, of course, sir!"

"You will hear from my associate tomorrow. On this phone." He placed it on the bar and turned to leave.

"Sir, why me?"

The Armani suit kept walking toward the door as he flippantly called back a return, "You know how to follow orders without asking questions—from now on."

A love-hate relationship began that next morning for a job he could never have dreamed he'd have. All he had to do was drive these crazy, scripted routes for this crazy, cold woman. He was paid a thousand bucks a day. This compensated for her foul moods, quirky ways and even her abusive responses to the rare times he forgot and questioned or "interfered."

The worst infraction had cost him a weekend in "the room". He'd been sitting at the bar drinking with his buddies when one of them asked him where he was working now.

He told him about the mysterious company and his nice fat paycheck. He told him about the Armani Suit and the Crazy Carpet Bagger. And just as he was about to tell him about the red door in the high security building, someone came up from behind and hit him upside the head with a bottle. When he woke up it was in "the room." Their head of security taught him to shut up then. He'd never told anyone anything about his job since. No one. Nothing.

He made more money than he could spend as a simple bachelor and had never trusted banks. He hid all of his wealth in nondescript boxes behind a false wall in the back of his walk-in closet. The only family he had was an ailing mother staying at St. Mary's Home for the Aged and Infirmed, where he paid handsomely for her to have the best room, best care, best food. She didn't recognize him anymore, but he visited her nonetheless, every Sunday afternoon. He introduced himself to her as an orderly at the hospital, they watched an hour of television together, and he shook her hand gently before excusing himself to "get back to work."

His clothing reflected his wealth, but that was because it was part of his uniform as an employee of Armani. He couldn't say he was proud to work for the Overseas Franchise Administration company, but he certainly had grown accustomed to the money.

All this played through his head as he walked slowly down the brightly lit corridor here on the fiftieth floor. His shoes clicked smartly on the polished marble floor. Passing an ornate mirror, he stopped to quickly adjust his tie again and smoothed back the hair above his ears that escaped his cap. He took a deep breath and walked on to the end of the hallway where one lone door stood. It was open.

Hesitating to cross the threshold without invite, he tentatively stopped in the doorway. "Hello?"

"Come in, Dickerson. Keep your hat on, do not remove your coat or gloves, and touch nothing. Sit." He sat in the chair across from a large oak desk. Behind it sat the heavily scented Armani, his elbows casually resting on the wooden top, manicured fingers laced calmly together, chin resting on thumbs. "We have a situation. It is outside of your usual skill set and pay scale, but you have shown yourself to be reliable over the past seven years and so we are sure you will be able to handle it with the utmost discretion."

"Yes, sir. Of course."

"Should you have difficulty in carrying out our request to the fullest, we will have to consider consequences. They will include immediate termination. Is that understood?"

"Sir, I'd hate to lose my job."

"I'm not talking about your job."

Unexpectedly, anger boiled up inside Dickerson and he half stood, blurting, "Wait a minute, are you threatening my life?"

"Calm down. No, of course not. Dickerson, how is your mother doing these days? I have heard that people in homes are vulnerable to accidental falls and sometimes have unexpected medical complications. Have you found this to be true?"

Realization settled in and Dickerson sat dejectedly back into the chair. "Yes, sir. That is true. But I will do anything to protect and help her."

"Very good. Now, when we picked up a package earlier today there were certain, well, issues which we were not aware of. Because of these problems, we will not be able to capitalize on our specific investment, so we need you to take care of the package. Understood?"

"Um, not exactly, sir. You want me to bring it back?"

"NO!" It was the Armani's turn to rise out of his chair. "You must dispose of the package in a way and place that no one, including me, knows about. It must be permanent and it must be immediate. I want absolutely nothing to tie back to our company in this. Can you do this, or can you not?"

"Yes, sir. I understand now, sir. I will take care of it right away." Dickerson was flustered enough at the Armani's uncharacteristic outburst to have the sense to respond without thinking. He was a yes man and he had an important job to do for this company. He could do it without thinking, like he was paid to do it.

Armani sat back down, "You will be paid five times your normal rate and it shouldn't take you long. Enjoy your visit with your mother on Sunday."

"Thank you, sir." He stood to go. "Where is the package?"

"There you go, asking questions again. I really thought we were done with that type of behavior. Perhaps another visit to "the room" is in order?"

"No, sir! I'm sorry. I just...."

"You will find the package wrapped and ready to be taken out in the trunk of your car. It is your concern now, I wash my hands of the whole affair. As far as I'm concerned, this conversation never happened. Understood?"

"Completely, sir. Thank you, sir."

"Now, I have other matters to attend to. Keep your gloves on when you push the elevator buttons." With that the Armani stood and strode out a door on the side of the room that Dickerson hadn't noticed. And Dickerson sat alone, his head swirling.

"You heard the man, get the hell out of here and do your job." The raspy voice made him jump. She sat on the other side of the room, reading her thick paperback.

"Yes, ma'am, right away, ma'am." He stood and marched quickly toward the door.

"And Dickerson?" she rasped.

"Yes, ma'am?"

"Don't fuck this up."

"Yes, ma'am."

With that he retraced his steps down the echoing corridor and down the elevator and out the red door. Frank met him halfway to his car and whispered, "She's gonna have you take care of the baby. Here's a card." Frank slipped it into Dickerson's left front pocket behind his little black planner.

"Take care of what? What's going on? What are you talking...?"

"Shhhh, they can't know I talked to you about it. Just take it there, okay?" Dickerson glanced at him as he fumbled with his car keys in the ignition. Frank raised an eyebrow and patted the left side of his own chest twice before turning to man the red door again.

Dickerson cleared the gate before he allowed himself to think about what cargo lay in his trunk and what deal he'd just made with the devil. He pulled over, rested his forehead on the steering wheel and cried.

He drove around most of the night, caught in indecision. On one hand he needed a plan for what to do with the problem in his trunk, which would be immediate and permanent. On the other hand he fumed and resented the trap he was in. He hadn't signed up for this—he was a driver, not a garbage man. And the man who'd lived in his skin prior to "the room," prior to the seven years he'd lived as a yes man, prior to doing unthinkable things without thinking, prior to his conscience being numbed by the money and the mechanical nature of his job, well, this man was still alive, though barely. And this prior man had priorities, too. Family, work ethic, being able to face himself in the mirror. He somehow knew this night would be a crossroads. Tonight would put a nail in the coffin, but he wasn't sure whose it would be. Either that of his mother or his self-respect.

He drove out of the city into open countryside, searching for the overgrown entrance he hadn't seen since he was a kid. Finding it, he barreled through a small rusted chain and up the rutted dirt road that had been carved through the trees of the thick forest. He entered a clearing of sorts, devoid of trees but overgrown with tall prairie grasses and scraggly bushes. Here he made his way to and pulled over at the edge of an old quarry. He'd made his decision with the desperation of a man trapped by circumstances out of his control. He stepped out of the car and peered over the edge. Dark blue water in the bottom assured him of a depth that would hide the remains of his car permanently. This quarry had been long ago abandoned, mined of its treasures and stripped of its usefulness. The symbolism was not lost on Dickerson as he thought of his own life and what he'd become. This was the only act that made sense to him. His mother would be spared because he'd dispose of the package as they asked him to. And he'd finally be free of them in the only way he ever could be.

That would be it then. He'd drive his ill-gotten car into the quarry and disappear off the face of the earth. Because no matter how hard he tried to deny it, no matter how quiet he'd been and stupid he'd acted, no matter how much of a yes man, he'd known. He'd known what those packages really were. He'd known they'd been taken from choices of desperation and forced into lives of desperation. He'd known he was a pawn in this game and suddenly no amount of sterile thinking could erase the malignant truth of what he'd done, what he'd become. The only way he could possibly live with himself now would be to rid the world of himself, to throw a wrench in the cogs of the sinister machine he worked for. A temporary wrench, yes, for there would be other drivers, other yes men, others who would be numbed by money, silenced by fear, sanitized into separating their actions from their identity. But he would slow it, and more important, he would be done.

Buoyed by the new sense of heroism rising up in his chest, he went back to the car and backed it up one-hundred feet, perpendicular to the edge of the quarry. His plan was to push the pedal down all the way until he reached it. He imagined himself soaring across and landing miraculously on the other side, like in the action movies he watched at home alone. Shaking his head back into reality, he pushed the power button on his stereo and readied himself to turn up the CD. Jazz had been the soundtrack of his life and it would sure as hell be the soundtrack of his death. But it jammed.

"Oh, shit!" he muttered aloud. The CD player was in the back of the car, in the compartment with the package in it, in the trunk. There was no way he was going to go back there and open that thing up. It made more sense to take his last flight in silence. He backed the car up another hundred feet and sat with the engine idling. He forced himself back into anger, tensing his muscles and replaying every wrong done to him in his fifty-three years of life. The slaps of a cruel father, the passivity of a helpless mother, the rejection at the altar by his high school sweetheart. Most of all, the seven years of working for the evil empire, being slighted, shut up, emasculated, demeaned, demoralized, dehumanized. He was done.

"Damn you!" he shouted to them all and pushed down hard on the accelerator. The engine roared forward, and he heard the package in the trunk thud against the back of the car. He pushed down harder, his teeth clenched against the scream trying to rip out of his throat. But he heard it. The scream shocked him into pushing on the brake. The car skidded to a shaky stop in the gravel just before the edge of the quarry and Dickerson sat, staring and breathing in time to his rapidly beating pulse. It took a full minute for him to register that it wasn't his scream. It was coming from the back of the car. It was coming from the baby. He glanced back and saw why he could hear the cries so distinctly — one of the back seats had been folded down, opening a hole directly to the trunk.

He thought about just pushing over the edge anyway but knew he couldn't do it with the sound of a terrified infant ringing in his ears. It quickly got under his skin and he had to make it stop. One way or another.

He popped the trunk and tore open his car door. He marched angrily to the back of the car and threw up the trunk lid. There it was, face mashed into the fine carpet, crying and gasping for breaths. He rolled it over quickly and saw a tiny snot and drool smeared face. He picked the bundle of dirty blankets up and held the infant close to his chest, his tears flowing freely now. The baby was alive!

This was a game changer, for sure. Part of him wanted to save its life, but he couldn't just take it home and care for it. They'd find out. The first thing he needed to do was get it out of the cold wind. He sat down in the front seat of the car and held it against his left shoulder until the crying stopped. Mentally coming up with and rejecting option after option, he finally came to the only conclusion that made sense. He had to follow through with his plan to finish them both off in the quarry. Feeling much more defeated than heroic now, he shifted into reverse and got into position again. He glanced down at and saw to his dismay that his shirt pocket was soaked with thick white spit up. He knew his planner would be ruined and insanely wondered how he'd be able to do his job without it. He laughed out loud as he remembered that his impending homicide/suicide would probably have worse consequences on his resume than a soggy planner.

With new resolve, he rolled down his window to feel the wind in his face, held onto the baby, stepped on the gas, released the wheel, and laughed wildly as the car careened toward the cliff. His last frantic act this side of the crossroads was to pull out the wet, matted planner from his breast pocket, glance at the little white card stuck to its back cover, and throw them out the window. He realized as the car jumped over the edge and free fell to the water below that he, too, was finally free.

## CHAPTER TWO

# The Loose Ends

He hated lying to her, he really did. But there really wasn't any other choice, was there. He wasn't at all the person she thought she'd married. He wasn't even sure whether he was a good guy or a bad guy anymore. Probably a bad guy. Good guys don't keep secrets from their beautiful, adoring wives.

His keys he threw absently into the little bowl in the entry way. "Honey, it's just me!" He liked to announce himself so that she wouldn't be startled when he walked in the door. Sometimes she was heavily involved in her meditations or whatever they were and he hated to interrupt. Today was one of those days.

"I'll be out in a minute, Frank." He heard her muffled voice from the bedroom and went to the fridge to grab a beer. Thirty seconds later he was sitting in front of the TV, prepared to finish the night in his chair, hoping he wouldn't have to answer too many questions because, man, he really did hate lying to her. Especially lately.

She came in a couple minutes later and greeted him with a kiss on the cheek. "Supper's in the microwave, babe. Want me to bring it in here again?"

"Sure."

"How was your day?"

"Oh, fine. Nothing exciting. Pretty boring, actually." He tried to shrug her off.

"Did you see your employers today? Will they give you the time off for our vacation?"

"Um, no, I didn't see them today, must not have been there. I'll try tomorrow."

"Okay. Well maybe tomorrow you'll get that chance."

He nodded assent and flipped through the stations. This was their nightly routine and it comforted him. Her, not so much. She'd been prying more, gently and slowly asking about things which he supposed every wife had a right to know. But he wouldn't, couldn't tell her. It was for her own protection. His secrecy was causing a rift, but his honesty would cause a much larger one, he was sure.

She brought him a tray with his supper on it, a steaming bowl of stew, thick piece of homemade buttered bread and another bottle of Miller. "Thanks, honey."

"I got a strange phone call today, Frank."

"Oh?" he garbled through a mouthful of bread, eyes fixed on the screen ahead where the talking heads were discussing the Colts' chances for the playoffs.

"Yes, I think it may have been about your employer."

He snapped the TV off, choked down his bite of food with a loud gulp and turned to face her. "Really? What did they say?"

"Well, it was a woman and she asked me if I was the wife of Frank Longly. Then she asked me if I knew anything about what you did for a living. I said, of course, he does security downtown. She said you might be in trouble, that we needed to leave town. Then she hung up, Frank."

Frank sat in shock. It was true, he was in more trouble than she knew.

He gestured using his pointer finger in front of his mouth, pleading with his eyes for her to be quiet. Then he scribbled on a piece of scratch paper: *Only say "yes, of course."* She nodded, and then he spoke. "Honey, I appreciate your concern. You know I work for an investment company who buys and sells in foreign markets. This was just a scare tactic by a competitor to try to make you worry and make me want to leave my company. But you can't scare me that easily." He waited.

"Yes, of course, dear. How silly of me."

"Let's take a drive after dinner. We can put the top down and go get some ice cream."

"Of course. Sounds wonderful, dear." She nodded knowingly and stroked his wedding ring finger gently, her eyes full of questions. She silently searched his for answers.

An hour later they were flying out of town, hair mussed in the wind and Creedence Clearwater Revival blasting on the stereo of Frank's '67 Fastback. When they got to Pokhant River he found a parking place and asked her if she wanted to go for a walk with him. "Of course!"

"You can lock your purse in the trunk, you won't need it."

"Are you sure?" He shook his head wildly for her to be quiet and nodded. "Oh, I'm sure you are right, love. Of course I won't need it."

He shut the trunk door and they walked hand in hand to the river's edge before he spoke again. "I just want to hold you, dear." He pulled her close and began to touch her. First, under the collar of her jacket, then inside her pockets. He unzipped her coat, reached in and touched the pockets of her blouse. She stood awkwardly as he felt around the waistband of her pants and reached down into her pants pockets. He bent and ran his thumb around the cuffs of her slacks. He gently lifted first one shoe and then the other, examining the underside of each. Satisfied, he stood and wrapped his arms around her, pulling her into an embrace. She let herself melt into his chest, and then the tears came for both of them. His rapidly beating heart told her all she needed to know. He loved her, he was in trouble, and her prayers were needed.

"I gave him the card you gave me." He whispered into her ear as he stroked the hair on the back of her head.

"Gave who what card?"

"My co-worker was in trouble today, and you told me it was for people who were in trouble."

She pulled away and looked up into his eyes, "Frank, what are you talking about, dear?"

"That card for your church or whatever. I had it in my pocket from Sunday and when I realized it was a baby I didn't even think about it really. I just handed it to my co-worker. I stuck it in his shirt pocket and I told him to take it there."

"Baby? Frank, what are you involved in?"

"I don't really know, babe. I probably don't want to. Usually I just guard a building and watch people go in and out. Mostly my two employers, but today was different. Today there was a recall. One of the packages wasn't what they wanted, so they brought it back out and she told me to put it in my co-worker's trunk, the trunk of his personal car. Then she dumped it into my arms and turned and went back inside. I grabbed it with one hand and jimmied the lock with the other hand."

"Wait a minute. Packages? What are you talking about?"

"The big woman I work for brings them in. I don't know where she gets them. I didn't know what they were, what they had to do with investment banking. And I never saw them leave. I'm not dumb, I knew they were doing something illegal, but I didn't know what they were, Lola. I swear! I figured they were dealing drugs or something and I couldn't tell you about any of it. I had to protect you!" He broke into sobs then. Slumping down to the ground, he cried into his hands. His shoulders shook with the effort. Lola knelt and held him silently, letting him release his sorrow.

When he'd regained control he looked up shamefully into her soft eyes. His voice cracked, "I saw this one. When I went to put the bundle into the trunk, part of the blanket snagged on the latch. It pulled off and I flipped it back over quickly, but I glimpsed it, Lola, a little closed eye. It was a baby." An anguished cry escaped him then, "Oh, God! They were babies, Lola. Babies." He bent his head back down and shook it, moaning in pain. "All of those bundles were babies and I never knew. I don't know what they do with the babies. And the one I put in that trunk—what have I done? Oh God, what have I done?" He wept into her arms.

"Frank, you didn't know they were babies. And I'm sure you did the right thing giving him that card. They will know how to help. Oh, dear, God will make a way out of this for you. I've been praying nonstop for you. I knew you were in trouble. Oh, Frank. I love you so much and you are not alone, my love." She just held him and stroked his hair as he sobbed.

The tears ran out and they found themselves sitting alone on the bank of the Pokhant, watching the sun go down. They watched a mallard duck and his hen who'd swum eagerly across the water toward them, hoping for a handout, swim back toward their nesting place. Further upriver a muskrat cut a path through the water on his way to his camouflaged house in the reeds. Still they both sat in silence. He lost in thought, she praying furtively. It came automatically to her now. It's what she did. And now she was seeing the beginnings of prayers answered, of movement in a stagnant marriage and answers to her searching questions. Not that she could celebrate these answers, for they were hard ones, and they unlocked even more questions.

Frank cleared his throat and began, "Lola, I can't leave the company, not yet. I know how high security they are.

They have others who watch over me, over us. That's why I checked you so thoroughly. That's why we left your purse in the car. Any time you are in public you are accessible for them to bug you. We cannot talk in our vehicles or in our home. I will find that way out you were talking about, and I will take it. But until then, I have to keep going to work and doing my job exactly the way I have been doing it. It's the only way to keep you safe."

"I'm not concerned about my safety, Frank."

"Well I am! And another thing, I need to find out more about these people I work for. Maybe I can somehow put a stop to what they are doing, but I won't be any help to anybody if I'm dead."

"Frank, I think God has you there for a reason."

"I don't know about all that God stuff, but one thing I know is that I am on the inside of something really big and I've never been one to shy away from something just because I'm scared."

"That's right, and you have my support one-hundred percent." She risked a smile and was rewarded with his grim smile in return.

"I know, babe." He was quiet again, holding her hand in his as she sat close to his side and rested her head on his shoulder. "I was just wondering about that phone call you got. Who was it? What do they want? Don't talk to anybody, honey, 'cause my company has ears everywhere. Could even have been them trying to see how much you know."

"I won't say a thing, honey."

"That's my girl."

"Should we go to the police?"

"No! I'm certain they wouldn't find any evidence. These people are very rich, thorough and incredibly secretive. I'm not even sure they haven't paid off city officials. It just doesn't make sense to me yet, any of it."

"Do you have any idea what your co-worker did with the baby?"

"No, hopefully he brought it to safety. I'm sure going to check into that next time I see him. Poor guy. I don't think he has any idea how much trouble he's in, too. He's just a driver, you know."

"Well, we just have to keep praying and hoping. It's out of our hands."

"Yep, you do that, honey. Seems to be stirring the pot already." He stood up and offered her a hand to pull herself up off the ground as well. They walked back to the car hand in hand and he unlocked the trunk so she could get her purse. She turned to go to her car door but he grabbed her and kissed her solidly, passionately on the lips before smirking and releasing her. She grinned back, feeling closer to him than she had in years. He'd let her into his secrets.

Frank arrived at work the next morning at 6:00 AM, freshly showered, shaved and dressed in his usual confidence, but inside his stomach churned. He wasn't sure how he could stand by as the Suit and the Bag Lady continued on with business as usual. He imagined himself confronting them in a million little scenarios that all ended badly—for him and his wife, not for this dark duo. In the loneliest hours of the night as he lay holding Lola close, he'd even considered running away with her. But in the light of day he knew again how futile that would be. They had resources beyond his understanding. They wouldn't stop until they found him, and he knew they would hurt his pretty wife badly. He'd heard about their security tactics and rumors about what was hidden deep inside the carpet bag.

So, his only option was to continue this farce. He willed himself to remain calm and stand at his guard post. And when his boss's car pulled in and parked at the usual time in his usual spot, he willed himself to escort him in with a smile, "Good day, sir." Suit grunted in return and walked through the red door.

Most of Frank's day was spent in a little booth, watching state of the art screens that channeled camera views from around the parking lots and red door. His job was to secure this parking pad and especially the red door. There were other security personnel inside who policed the interior. He had no contact with these people. He'd only met the head of security once and would prefer to never have contact with the man again if possible. Frank had actually gotten a dark chill down his backbone.

He was responsible for escorting Suit and Bag Lady to and from the door. Yesterday, Dickerson had been the only change in protocol he'd experienced in the three years he'd worked here. He'd often thought the company was either quite paranoid or he was missing something, because he really couldn't understand why they paid him so much to guard a hidden door. It had been a boring job, but his compensation had been more than adequate.

Suit always arrived first, promptly at 6:30 AM. The Bag Lady, however, was more of a wild card. Dickerson brought her at any hour of the day, always with a package stuck inside her old brown paisley carpet bag. Sometimes they came on the night shift. There was a guard then, too, but Frank had never spoken to him. Standard procedure was for Frank to clock out at 6:00 PM and stand directly by the red door as the night guard clocked in at the guard station. Most he'd done was tip his hat at the incoming guy before taking the stairs to his own car on the next level, where all employees parked except for Suit and the Bag Lady, of course. He had no idea when either of them left either. The Suit had never left before the end of Frank's shift.

So he had no way of knowing if Dickerson would be arriving with the Bag Lady today or not. He waited, scanning the screens, walking the perimeter of the lot, absently fingering the red door handle. He ate his lunch, alone, as usual, in his station surrounded by glass. He worked a crossword puzzle, browsed through his *Car and Driver* magazine, listened absently to seventies music on his old Panasonic radio, and scanned the grounds again and again and again. He'd become a master at occupying his mind in the face of a job that had very little action.

Today he worked even harder to fill his thoughts with something, anything other than the glimpse of a sweet sleeping eye and soft cheekbone of a beautiful little baby wrapped in rags. But his thoughts replayed the event over and over. How light the baby was as he placed it gently into the trunk of the car. He'd made sure to place it facing up and he'd reached in and quickly punched the rear seat forward so there'd be plenty of air in there. Before closing the door he'd reached in and moved that loose flap of cloth away from the baby's face so it would be unobstructed. All this he did even though he didn't even know if the baby was alive. He didn't have time to check. Cameras were watching.

It was 5:45 when Suit walked out the red door. Surprised, Frank stood up and walked briskly to him, "Everything all right, sir?"

Suit stopped and studied Frank's face for a minute. "Take a ride with me, Frank?" The question was more of an order.

"Of course, sir." He nodded at the incoming security guard.

Suit nodded toward the passenger seat of his new car and strode to the driver's side. Frank obediently got in. The unmistakable cologne smell permeated the interior, an invisible aromatic fog. The key turned in the ignition, Tchaikovsky music filled the space. Suit turned it up as he drove out of the garage and out of the city. Frank got the message and sat silently watching out the window as familiar landmarks passed by. Within twenty minutes they were out of the densely populated city, within thirty they were in corn fields.

Suit slowed down and turned the music off. After a few minutes of silence he turned toward Frank and asked him, "Do you like working for us, Frank?"

"Of course, sir," he half-lied. He really did like the pay and the hours. He really didn't like the mystery or the way his stomach was in knots at the moment. What was Suit planning on doing with him?

"Good, because I was just thinking that it would be difficult to replace you. There are so few men who could be trusted to stay focused on such a menial job without getting bored or nosy. I have been generally satisfied with your performance, Frank."

So maybe he wasn't bringing him out here to get rid of him after all? "Thank you, sir."

"Something very unfortunate happened yesterday, Frank. As you know, one of our packages was not what we'd ordered and needed to be handled delicately. We appreciate your discretion in the matter and how promptly you handled things. Usually I would have had my head of security handle such matters, but he was away on other business."

"Yes, sir."

"Let me get to the point. You are wondering, I am sure, why we are driving out here. Dickerson's car is somewhere nearby. He is not answering his phone and we fear something may have happened to him."

"Oh, I'm sorry to hear that, sir. How were you able to locate his car?"

"That's really none of your concern, now is it? We have our ways. Frank, I brought you along because you were the last person to touch that package."

"Sir?"

"Your fingerprints are all over it and I'm not sure what

Dickerson has done with it, but if it's in the wrong hands the trail will lead back to you. I figured you would want to make sure it was disposed of properly so as to avoid any possible misunderstandings from arising."

The realization of why Suit had brought him along hit Frank in the stomach like a punch. He was going to have to finish the job; the Suit needed him to do the dirty work so that he could keep his hands clean of it. And afterward he assumed the head of security would be paying him a visit to keep him quiet. Frank's only hope of escape rested in the fact that the Suit didn't know Frank was aware of what lay inside the old rags, so he played this up. "Oh, well, I'll help in any way I can, sir. I know how imperative it is to keep any trade secrets out of the hands of our competition."

"Good man." Frank didn't feel at all like a good man. He felt trapped and ashamed. But he knew he had to play along. He had to get more information. He had to get himself and Lola out of this mess. He had to. But he had no clue how.

Suit turned then, onto an old rutted dirt road. It twisted a mile through thick woods, then abruptly cleared on the other side of the tree line. Suit pulled up short and stopped the car. He threw it into park and stepped out. Frank took his cue and got out, joining Suit at the edge of a large drop-off. The dark blue water at the bottom of the pit could have been a mile deep for all he knew. They were in an old quarry. Looked like it had been abandoned for years except for a strange set of double car tracks that went from about two-hundred yards back near the tree line straight ahead toward the giant hole carved out of rock in front of them.

Frank imagined it plummeting. He could tell by the tracks that it had been no accident, that Dickerson had probably lost his nerve on his first attempt. He imagined the baby rolling around in the trunk, and mentally channeled the pain and anger that rose up into a little spot in his conscious mind where a vigilante was being fed. He would bring these people down one way or another.

An insane thought flashed through his mind: what if he just pushed the man over the edge right now? He was pretty sure he had the physical strength advantage, and the Suit wouldn't be expecting it. He stepped nearer the man, visualized shoving him with both hands, his plummet broken only by angry yells and finally a splash below. Even the daydream gave him satisfaction. Until he thought of the big woman who'd be left behind. The woman with deranged, cold eyes who'd carry on the twisted trade. He'd be no closer to finding out what these people were really involved in, he'd be no closer to keeping his wife safe. He stuck his hands in his pockets and willed himself to relax his tensed body. Not yet, Frankie, he thought to himself. Not yet.

"That's it, then," Suit casually turned and headed toward his car. Frank watched him, wishing he'd had the courage to wipe the smugness off the man's face once and for all. He followed obediently after him.

Out of the corner of his eye it caught his attention, glinting sunlight. Left of the tire tracks the car had made, lying on the scraggly grass—a little black book. Recognizing it as Dickerson's, Frank strode over and picked it up, turning it over in his hand. He opened it and saw the alternating red and blue X's. Nothing else.

"What have you found?" Frank jumped inside at the Suit's voice. He hadn't seen him walk up.

"Looks like a planner of some sort." He handed it over.

The Suit paged through it, then, apparently satisfied there was nothing incriminating in it, no names, no places, strode to the pit to send it flying over.

Frank turned to go to the car. That's when he saw it. A little white piece of cardstock lay on the ground, partially obscured by dust and gravel. It was turned downward, but he knew what it said, "Sparta Baptist Church. Reverend Philips" He knew if he reached down to pick it up the Suit would question him so he casually kicked a rock on top of it and walked on. Both men climbed into the new model Bentley, otherwise identical to the one Dickerson had rolled off the roof of the parking garage seven years before, and the Suit reached to start the engine. Before turning the key, he gave Frank a long, hard look. "I'm sure I don't have to tell you that discretion is absolutely essential, as always."

"No sir, I understand, sir." Frank's heart pounded loudly in his ears, fearing he'd been spotted hiding the business card.

"Just go about your business and forget what you even saw here."

"Of course sir, no problem." But he would never forget what he'd seen this day, or yesterday. He would remember and recall every detail to the proper authorities at the proper time. What's more, he would have much more to hand over. Evidence, witnesses.

They drove the rest of the way to the office in silence. The Suit dropped him at his car, "Frank, you have done well for us the last two days. You will be well compensated."

"Yes, sir, thank you sir."

"And Frank?"

"Yes, sir?"

"Just a little advice from one man to another. When you promise your wife something, you really should follow through. Take ice cream, for example. Seems like a minor enough thing, but when you don't do what you say you are going to do, it gets people to wondering, you know. I just would hate for people in your life to doubt your word, or get insecure in their dealings with you, you understand."

"I understand, sir." Now Frank's stomach dropped. He understood the veiled threat to his wife, the reassurance that yes, they were being listened to, watched, scrutinized. He set his jaw resolutely, gripped his steering wheel and raced to be with Lola. If he'd known what awaited him at home he wouldn't have hurried. He probably would have avoided going there altogether. And he definitely would have pushed that smug bastard off the side of the cliff.

That morning Lola had kissed Frank out the door and immediately gone to her room to pray. She spent hours like this each day, but today there was an added intensity and fervor to her requests of God to protect and lead Frank. And today she prayed for a baby she'd never met to be rescued.

Mid-morning she was lying face-down on her bed,

unsure how else to pray, when a quiet but firm voice in her head told her to *get up and go to the church, right now.* It was the same voice that had first told her to *pray hard for Frank* months ago. She'd obeyed then and she obeyed now.

As she drove the twenty-five blocks to Sparta Baptist Church, Lola reached over to grab her phone out of her purse to call Reverend Phillips and let him know she was coming and that Frank was in danger. But it wasn't there. She had grabbed her keys on the way out the door, but left her little bag behind, sitting on the kitchen table. After considering whether to go back for it, she remembered the directive, *"right now,"* and kept driving toward the church. She mentally rehearsed what she would say to the church office receptionist. "Hi, I'm Lola and I attend this church and I think I've been sent here on some sort of mission from God but I don't know what it is." And to Reverend Phillips, "My husband is in trouble and I think you can help me but I'm not sure how yet." Even in her head it came out awkward and uncomfortable.

Lola parked and entered the main door of the church where she was a faithful attender, had been for the last year, but was still unknown. When she and Frank had moved to this side of town she'd seen a flyer at the grocery store advertising a women's brunch held here. Hoping to make friends, she'd gone. And been disappointed. The women already had friends and didn't seem to be interested in making any new ones. Lola had gone home feeling invisible and discouraged.

But she'd gone back Sunday and instantly was

impressed with Reverend Phillips. He taught straight from the Bible, which she rarely heard anyone do anymore. He was compassionate and wanted the church to reach out more, get involved in causes, get to know the needs of their surrounding community. It was a very large, diverse congregation and Lola often daydreamed about what they could accomplish for the Kingdom of God if they'd initiate. Reverend Phillips was a charismatic teacher. During his sermons the congregation seemed moved—to tears, to hearty "Amens!," to filling up the offering plates, even. But not to action. They shuffled back out the same way they'd shuffled into the tall, wide doors of the entrance— individuals preoccupied with their own needs and wants.

Frank didn't attend church with her, so there was no reason anyone would know or care about him. The reverend probably had never even noticed her in the congregation of five-hundred. She'd been reluctant to try any other small groups after the women's brunch ordeal. She'd considered trying another church, but seemed drawn back into Sparta Baptist at least for one more week. One more week had turned into fifty-two and she'd gone from a woman looking for social connection to a woman deeply connected to God. She read His Word, spent increased amounts of time in His presence, and heard His still small voice. So, despite her lack of relationships in this building, she walked in—a woman on an unspecified yet urgent mission.

She stated her name to the receptionist, asked to see the reverend and took a seat sandwiched between a tall potted plant and a short table covered in magazines. *Guideposts,*

*Our Daily Bread, Christianity Today*. None of them sparked her interest as she sat rigidly, hands clenched together on her lap to stop the nervous impulse to pick at her fingernails. She heard the receptionist speak into a phone, "Reverend Phillips, there is a woman to see you. No, she doesn't have an appointment in my book. Yes, I'll tell her."

Turning to Lola she said, "I'm sorry, the Reverend is dealing with a crisis right now and won't be able to see you today. I'm very sorry."

Lola blurted out the first thing that came to her mind, "Actually, I do have an appointment. It was set up by God himself not more than fifteen minutes ago."

"I see. I'll let him know." Her doubtful tone wasn't lost on either of them. She spoke into the phone again, "Yes, she says she has an appointment and that it was made by God fifteen minutes ago. Do you want me to schedule her for tomorrow?"

Suddenly Reverend Phillips appeared at the door. "I've been waiting for you. Is Frank your husband?"

Surprised, Lola sputtered, "Yes, but how did you...?"

"Please come with me." The reverend led her back through the office suite, past the open door with "Reverend Phillips" on the etched nameplate and into a back hallway. He unlocked a nondescript door. Behind it was a metal staircase, which they descended three levels before reaching a second locked door.

Lola found herself in a private apartment, sparsely but comfortably furnished. Next to the farthest wall facing a colorful painting stood a tall man in a rumpled high-end jacket. Two things struck Lola immediately about his appearance. The first was that he was barefoot, and the second was that he was swaying back and forth and bouncing slightly on his heels. He kept making a shushing sound with his mouth and patting his chest. It made no sense to Lola until the reverend cleared his throat loudly and the man turned away from the wall to face them.

The man was holding a baby.

## CHAPTER THREE

# The Safe Room

Frank knew what his car could do. He'd had a long love affair with muscle cars and rebuilt the engine in his Mustang. That had been a hobby he and Lola had shared, actually, previous to the sadness overtaking them, before he'd gotten bored with life and begun lying to his wife. When he was home he wanted to hide from it, to hide from her. Their hobbies together forgotten, at least by him. But no more. He needed her.

He pushed the pedal as hard as he dared. He knew the local police would leave him alone. They had stopped pulling him over after the first few times. One look at the company ID clamped onto his jacket and they'd waved him on without even a warning. He'd thought it was just another perk of working for a large, powerful company in this town. Today it served him well. The RPMs jumped and his Mustang lunged forward through a green light. He'd been trying to call her ever since leaving Suit. He kept getting her voicemail. His messages were increasingly unable to hold back the panic in his voice. She always answered. Always.

He drove into the driveway and parked without pulling into the garage. Rushing to the front door, alarms went off in his head. The door was open, the doorjamb broken where a solid kick had splintered it. Frank instinctively went for his gun and pulled it out before entering his home. Someone had pulled every drawer out, pushed over cabinets, smashed his TV and ransacked every square inch that he could see. Nothing seemed to be missing. It looked like they'd been either searching for something or just trying to send a message to intimidate them. How unnecessary, Frank thought. He didn't have anything the company would want and he'd been scared into submission long ago. Not to mention being reminded of their ruthless power today, again.

But he didn't know where Lola was. He began a frantic search through the house, calling her name—his volume increasing until he was screaming it. Panic overtook him and his search became irrational, slamming doors, throwing down appliances and furniture. Exhausted, he slumped down in a pile of his wrecked home and began to sob, head on his knees, at a loss for what to do next. He should call the police. But he wasn't sure whose side they were on.

He lay down hopelessly on the linoleum and numbly surveyed his surroundings through blurry tears. Pieces of random items began to make sense to him. A prescription pill bottle, a small baggy of Kleenex, a silver compact, a small coin purse came into focus and then were highlighted when he realized what they were. These were the standard contents of his wife's purse. He rummaged around for more and came up with a lipstick case, broken handled hairbrush and a pack of gum.

As disconcerting as it was to see that her purse had been man-handled and dumped out unceremoniously, what he didn't see filled him with hope. Her cell phone was nowhere to be found.

She had it! And she couldn't answer the phone because she was shaken up and hiding somewhere. Or she'd turned it off so they wouldn't find her if it rang or vibrated. Or it had run out of battery and she couldn't get to the charger. A host of scenarios flooded his mind and he clung to each of them with renewed confidence that he would find her, he would protect her, and he would never let her out of his sight again. Never.

He had to hear her voice. Surely she'd answer when she saw it was him calling again. Surely she'd had time to get to a safe place. Pulling out his phone and punching buttons automatically, he listened for the rings on the other end and waited expectantly to hear her voice.

Instead he felt a vibration on his foot. He looked down and saw a dishcloth dancing. Kicking it away, he furiously stomped on the cell phone hidden beneath, breaking it before it could confirm the unthinkable with an audible ring. She would have never gone anywhere without her phone, yet she had. She would have never voluntarily left him, yet she was gone. As he stood unsteadily in the middle of the trashed room he smelled it. The sickly sweet musk of a man used to excess lingered in the air—excess wealth, excess power, excess cologne.

Something inside Frank's mind snapped. It was like a guitar string being tuned higher and higher until it has no give left. Then the tuning peg is twisted a little more. And a little more. And TING, the string bounces around wildly.

If Frank had held it together a little longer he would have seen Lola's car keys were missing along with her car from out of the garage. If he'd been very observant he'd have seen her bright blue duffel bag missing from the top shelf of their closet, as well as the Colt .45 he stored hidden behind it. He also would have seen the hastily scribbled note written in lipstick on their master bathroom mirror, hidden behind the door he'd flung open in his frenzied search. FRANK, I'M OKAY. I'LL CALL SOON.

But as it was, all Frank saw through his blind rage was the basement steps, the combination to his gun safe, and the rifles and ammo he packed into the trunk of his car. These flashed before him like strobe lights in his darkness. The after-images, however, were unchanging. They were the faceless head of The Suit after he'd blown it away.

The baby had been crying the breath-hitching, hard cry of the truly distressed. Lola knew this because even though it was sleeping, every thirty seconds or so a heartbroken hiccup of breath and sigh would escape the tiny mouth. She'd seen this many times over the years she'd worked at the hospital. Back before the move to another side of town, before it was too difficult to work with babies anymore, before they'd given up trying for their own, before the sadness had enveloped her. Finding Sparta Baptist had been part of her new start in life, her purposeful journey out of personal darkness. She wondered sometimes if her dogged attendance was a way to prove that she wasn't mad at God. She knew Frank's refusal to come with her was because he was.

She walked to the man holding the swaddled child, "Poor thing's certainly had quite an eventful day, I'd wager."

He glanced at the reverend, got a reassuring nod and held the baby toward Lola. "Do you want to hold the baby? My arms are getting tired."

He transferred the bundle awkwardly to Lola's outstretched arms. She didn't realize she'd reached for the child until she felt its slight weight and pulled the warm body next to her chest. Driven by the longing she'd denied over the past year, yet afraid of the sadness gripping her heart again, compassion for this tiny newborn won and she held it close. "Is it a boy or girl?"

"Um, I kept the baby wrapped up. I didn't know what to do. It all happened so fast and I just kept walking and then I got here and it's all kinda blurry."

Reverend Phillips spoke up, "Mr. Dickerson, you are exhausted. Please sit down and rest. The baby is in good hands with Lola."

A very tired Dickerson slumped onto the couch and began mumbling, "Yes, so tired. But I did the right thing. Mother'd be proud of me. But I can't tell her. I can't go see her. I have to stay invisible now."

Lola stood nearby, swaying with the sleeping baby. Reverend Phillips sat on the coffee table across from Dickerson, and they were able to piece his story together through his paranoid offerings. He'd driven over the edge of the quarry with the baby, holding it tight to his chest before they hit the water. The impact threw him forward into the steering wheel and he heard something crack. He knew it was the baby's head. Mortified, he unbuckled his seatbelt, pushed his way out of the open window and swam up, kicking hard, holding the baby tight with one arm and blinking through the blood that swirled around his face. He made it to the surface and gulped in air before looking around the edge of the pond for a place to climb out. He found it on the far side, a road cut down to the quarry bottom for trucks and digging machinery to access the deep rock. He placed the baby on the ground, pulled himself up and lay there on the bank, catching his breath. He tasted blood, felt it gushing down his cheeks and neck. Relief replaced the horror of imagining the child with a broken skull. It was his nose that had broken. He reached over then to see if the baby was breathing. Had he suffocated it by holding it too close to himself? Or had it drowned by drinking in the murky water?

Dickerson stood, realized absently that he'd lost his shoes in the pond, and pulled the child up, patting its back. Water spurted out of the little mouth, and breathing followed. Relieved, he carried it like a football up out of the quarry while holding his other hand to his nose to stop the bleeding.

He'd walked miles in shredded socks before a farm

truck passed by him, slowed, turned around and pulled up next to him. "Are you alright, mister?" A teenage boy wearing a large cowboy hat sat behind the wheel.

"I need to get to Sparta Baptist Church." Dickerson was surprised that he'd remembered the name on the card. "Do you know where that is?"

"Yes, sir! I know exactly where that is. I got family who go there."

"I'm sorry but I can't pay you. I lost my wallet."

"No worries. Climb on in."

So the boy had driven them to the church and asked surprisingly few questions. He'd given Dickerson a rag to sop up the blood that was still trickling out of his nose, and pulled out an old blanket from behind the seat for them to cover themselves up in. He turned the heat on high so they could dry out a little and made small talk until they found themselves in front of Sparta Baptist. "You take care, mister."

"Thank you. Let me get your address so I can send you some money."

"No need. Just take good care of that young 'un there. She's something special."

They'd gone into the church and he asked to speak with the pastor. Reverend Phillips took one look at them and whisked them into his office for a quick explanation. He turned to Lola as she patted the sleeping baby's back softly. "I brought them down to this apartment only a half hour ago."

Lola asked him how he'd known she was coming. "I got these two down to the safe room and then I went up to my office to call the police. Just as I reached for my phone I heard a voice in my head, *Stop. Don't call. Frank's wife will help.* And then a few minutes later my secretary told me you were in the waiting room."

"You can't call the police, Pastor. They'll figure out what I've done and come after us. And my mother."

"And Frank," Lola chimed in.

"Well, we have this safe room for a reason. The founders of this church were involved in the Underground Railroad. They dug out hiding places for escaping slaves with their bare hands. Then, during the Cold War, members were paranoid enough to secure this underground bunker and stock it with clothing and food. We've kept it upgraded over the past decade for domestic violence situations and the like. We can set you and the baby up here for a while until we figure out what to do next. I can go get some diapers and clean blankets from the storage room, but we don't have any infant clothing or formula, I'm afraid."

"I'll go get those. I know what we'll need. We need to doctor up your nose, too, Mr. Dickerson."

Reverend Phillips excused himself to get the stuff for the baby and a change of clothing for Dickerson. Dickerson gave Lola a helpless look. "I don't know anything about babies, I'm afraid."

"I know, it's okay. Why don't you go get a nice warm shower and I'll have Reverend Phillips leave your change of clothing in on the bed. Looks like you could use that bed, too. I'll take care of the baby."

Relief spread across his face as Dickerson turned to go to the bathroom. The reverend returned with blankets and diapers. When he went to put the change of clothes in the other room, Lola set the baby on the couch and began to unwrap it. First was the blanket stained by Dickerson's nosebleed, and red soil from the quarry. The next layer in was soggy and tinged with yellow stains from a diaper well past its breaking point leaking through. The hospital receiving blanket was putrid. The baby had soiled itself, the hospital diaper had swollen up to five times its normal size with water from the lake and was disintegrating. Lola removed the diaper and smiled. She was a girl! Lola carefully wiped away the filth and put a new diaper on her. Then Lola began to remove the thin blanket wrapped around her little torso, intending to give her a little sponge bath and swaddle her in a fresh clean blanket from the church's stash. When she looked at what she'd unwrapped, Lola sat back in shock, her hand clamped to her mouth to stifle the gasp. It came out anyway, behind her, through the reverend who'd walked up to assist, "Oh, God!"

The baby had no arms.

Lola finished cleaning and wrapping up the baby. Dickerson came out freshly showered and wearing khaki pants that were a bit short and a button-up shirt that was a bit long. Exhaustion and stress etched his careworn face and Lola sent him to bed after asking him some questions about the baby and doing a cursory check of his broken nose. "The bleeding has stopped but it's still very swollen. My concern would be for loose bone fragments in your sinus cavity. We'll have to give it a couple more days of icing it down and see what we're working with."

Her exam of the baby complete, she discovered a new concern. Besides her obvious physical disability, Frank's account of their adventures of the day revealed a glaring problem. The baby had obviously been drugged heavily at the hospital and either the effects of the drugs had not fully worn off, had done permanent damage, or the infant was already showing signs of failure to thrive. She simply wasn't crying enough. She'd cried when she was rolled around in the back of the trunk. She'd cried when they'd arrived at the little safe room until Dickerson had lulled her back to sleep with his little sway/bounce dance. Other than that she'd been silent.

Lola knew that a hungry, cold, wet, soiled baby should be screaming nonstop until her needs are met. Hoping that it was just the after-effects of the sedative, she handed the baby to the reverend and set out to go get the formula this starving baby should be clamoring for.

First she had to go past her house to get her purse. Hurriedly she drove into the garage and ran through the kitchen door off of the garage. She was five steps in before it registered—her house was destroyed, ransacked. She saw in a glance that their valuables were still there, and knew. This was no home robbery. This was Frank's company trying to intimidate them. She stopped in her tracks and listened for signs that they were still there. Silence except for the thumping heartbeat in her chest. Walking room to room, she saw drawers pulled out, papers strewn, their belongings destroyed. Confused, she realized that the most out of place thing she observed in a house where everything was out of place was the scent in the air. It was a strong, earthy, minty smell, and it seemed to have landed in microscopic droplets on every square inch of her overturned home.

She quickly made the decision that her home wasn't safe to return to. She would pack a bag and stay at the safe room with the baby. She'd call Frank and tell him what had happened and tell him to join her. But she couldn't call him now, not when he was at work, not when he was being listened to. She ran into her bedroom and dug through the piles of clothing in haphazard piles and pulled out some for both of them. Looking for something to put them in, she went to their closet and reached up onto the top shelf to get her bag. Her outstretched fingers met with cold steel behind it and she absently grabbed the .45 Frank kept hidden there and threw it into the bag, too.

Next she ran to the kitchen, dropped the duffel by the door and searched for her purse. Its contents had been dumped onto the floor. She kicked around the objects that had once been her neatly organized home around until she came up with her credit card pocket book. She couldn't find her phone. The sudden thought that these people might return propelled her into panicked action. She tried to find a pen to write a note for Frank, but a couple seconds of frantic searching yielded nothing but her lipstick tube. She ran back into the master bathroom with it and wrote a quick message on the mirror.

Then she ran out the kitchen door with her bag in hand and drove to the store, asking God to protect her husband

and to give her the strength to hold it together long enough to get back to the church.

⌐∦⌐

Frank had no plan, really. Even if he had, it would have been impossible to execute with the blinding rage that fueled him. He drove to the building where he worked and sat in his car across the street, watching and waiting for something he couldn't fathom happening or him being able to create—an opportunity to kill the Suit. Night was falling now and he didn't know whether the man was even in the building. He had no security clearance to drive into the parking garage until morning. He decided to try to go to work the next day like normal, hoping to get a shot at the Suit when he came in at his usual time. Frank checked his phone, saw the battery was dead and decided not to even plug it in. Who would call him? Lola was gone. He snapped it shut, threw it down on the floor, reclined his seat and wasn't surprised when his dreams matched his waking nightmares.

⌐∦⌐

As soon as Lola reached the church, she'd called Frank from the church phone. It went right to voice mail every time, but she still tried every hour, hoping to hear him answer. He didn't, past the time he'd have returned from work, past the time he'd have eaten dinner, gone to bed. Worried now, she tried not to let her mind wander to what may have happened to him and used her energy to pray instead, and to care for the sweet baby God was using her to help rescue.

The infant had woken and begun screaming with a vengeance. The men were flustered and concerned, but Lola was relieved. She smiled and gave the baby some warm formula, which she drank in loud gulps until full, burped over Lola's shoulder and fell back into a satisfied sleep. This she repeated every few hours, the way a newborn should. Lola happily put her into a soft sleeper, changed her diapers through the night, and miraculously found snippets of sleep herself in between feedings. Dickerson crashed hard and the reverend went home for the night.

They planned to come together the next morning and figure out how to contact Frank and what to do with the baby. Surely there was a social service organization who would take her in? Lola dreamed about Frank finding her in the safe room, snuggling the baby in his arms and telling Lola, "This is our baby from God. She's something special."

Frank tried to smooth his rumpled uniform. He checked and rechecked his loaded pistol before tucking it back into its holster. He glanced at his face in the rear view mirror, tried to wipe the crazed look from his eyes, the haggard stubble from his chin, evidence of a deranged man who'd slept in his car. He drove into the parking garage at his usual time, cleared the security and walked down to his station to check in. He wasn't able to bring in his rifles, but he shouldn't need them. On a good day, Frank was an excellent marksman. This was not a good day, but he should be able to walk the Suit in and get off a shot at point blank range.

He walked up to the glass enclosed booth where the night guard he was to relieve was turned away from him—facing the time card machine, punching out, Frank assumed. When he opened the door to the booth, the man turned around and pushed a revolver against Frank's temple. "Let me just have that," the head of security reached into Frank's holster and took his gun. "Now let's go, Frankie." He led him in through the red door.

Lola woke to a gentle voice, "Good morning." Dickerson looked like a different man after a night of sleep. The swelling had gone down some on his nose. He was still black and blue around its bridge, but his eyes had lost their redness and were clear and bright. And sparkling. He nodded to her side and she saw why—the baby serenely sleeping, a smile on her little pink lips. She'd fallen asleep on the couch during the blur of feedings she'd taken during the night.

Dickerson handed her a cup of coffee as she carefully sat up without disturbing the infant. Reverend Phillips was sitting in a chair across from the coffee table, holding his own cup of steaming brew. He'd brought a bag of McDonald's breakfast for them, too.

"What time is it? I have to call Frank!" She dialed his number and was surprised when it didn't go right to voice mail. She waited, hope rising with each ring.

Relief flooded her when someone picked up, "Hello?"

Then doubt at the unfamiliar voice, "I'm sorry, I must have the wrong number. I'm trying to reach my husband."

"This is Frank's phone. Who is this?"

"This is his wife, can I speak to him?" Concern etched her voice now.

"Unfortunately, ma'am, I regret to inform you that your husband has been terminated." Click.

Lola sat stunned for a full minute, holding the phone in her hand, numbly staring at nothing. It dropped to the floor first, and she followed with a thud.

⌒∦⌒

Reverend Phillips and Dickerson made Lola comfortable on the bed and worked together to care for the baby. It took both of them to piece together how a diaper worked, how to make formula, how to hold her while burping. Lola slept most of the day, moaning Frank's name and tossing and turning. Whenever she did awake, she looked around wild-eyed, placed her surroundings and circumstances, rolled over into a fetal position and cried herself back to sleep. This went on for days.

Reverend Phillips began to spend more time in his office and attending church business, leaving Dickerson to watch over Lola and the baby. He offered food and water to Lola multiple times a day and succeeded in getting her to eat only with persistent and gentle coaxing, "Frank would want you to eat this, honey." "Frank would want you to keep living, dear."

He was equally gentle with the baby. "Little one, we need to give you a name." "You are so beautiful!" "There, there, my little lump of sugar, you are loved." His initial shock over seeing her deformity was very quickly replaced by a fatherly tenderness and fierce protectiveness. No matter what happened to this little girl, he would ensure it was what was the very best for her. He had helped her survive, now he aimed to make sure she got to live and thrive. He sang and waltzed around the room with her. He stroked her soft back, cradled her head in his large hand and whispered blessings to her. When he thought about the impossible beginning she'd had and the humiliation she'd likely experience throughout her life, he held her closer and wished beyond anything else there was a way to save her from it.

The men talked at length about their situation. Two men and a practically comatose woman in an underground bunker raising a disabled baby was less than ideal. No, this was temporary, but neither of them knew what to do next. Dickerson couldn't raise this child on his own. Besides being fairly clueless about parenting, cooking and housekeeping, he needed to maintain his pretend dead status in order to not become actual dead. Lola was a basket case. They didn't know how to contact her family or friends or how to help her out of her gut clenching sorrow. Reverend Phillips said God would make a way. In the meantime they waited, brainstormed, rejected idea after idea and were completely caught up in responding to the needs of a newborn.

Dickerson was surprised one day at lunchtime when Reverend Phillips bounded into the apartment excitedly. "We may have our answer!"

"What?"

"Yes, when I returned from visitations this morning my secretary told me about an appointment I have scheduled for this afternoon. It is with someone from a ministry called One for All. Have you heard of it?"

"No, what do they do?"

"Well, I'll find out more later, of course. But apparently they work in advocacy with young single mothers and provide out of state adoption placement. The representative goes to area churches to inform pastors of this resource."

"Wow, God works fast, don't he?"

"In my experience, Mr. Dickerson, God always works right on time," Reverend Phillips smiled, patted his new friend on the back, left lunch for them and excused himself to get back to work.

She was dressed neatly, her slim figure accented by her stylish suit, hair swept up into a loose bun. Reverend Phillips welcomed her into his office and sat comfortably across from her. She began, "Thank you so much for seeing me, Reverend Phillips. It really is a pleasure to meet you."

Her soft, lilting voice had a hint of an accent, Tennessee, maybe, Reverend thought. "You are very welcome. As you know we are a fairly large, diverse church. I am always interested in what community resources are available to my congregation."

"Yes, sir. Well, we are a ministry with many years' experience in helping young, under-supported mothers. We take them in under a confidential protection, provide for their medical care up to and through delivery of their children. For those who decide to give their baby the gift of adoption, we administrate these on a private basis."

"You mean closed adoption?"

"Yes. Our research and experience shows that this is what is best for the child in completing the transformation to their new lives and families. Especially since we specialize in cases where the mothers are unfit or unfortunate."

"Unfortunate?"

"That is the term we use for mothers who have not chosen their pregnancy. As you know, abortion is often regarded as a viable option, perhaps the only option for mothers who have been impregnated by rape or incest. Our organization seeks to provide another option. It is through confidential care of the mother and closed adoption."

"And how would I refer such a mother to you?"

"Here is my card," she handed him a card with the company logo One For All and her office number below it. "I hope we may be a valuable resource to your beautiful church."

"Thank you very much. Let me see you to the door." Reverend Phillips shook her hand and walked her out. Then he hurried down the steps to the safe room to tell Dickerson the good news. "I think these people really may be able to help us!" He filled him in on the details of the short meeting he'd had and waited expectantly for Dickerson's blessing.

Dickerson hesitated, however. "I don't know. I've been thinking, maybe I should keep her after all."

Reverend Phillips sat down across from him and began again, gently. "Now, we've been over this many times. You agreed that option may not be the best for her. She needs a stable family, people who don't have to hide from anyone. She will need special resources in order to compensate for her disability. It will be costly and time consuming for her parents to give her what she will need to overcome obstacles we haven't even considered. I know you want what's best for her, yet you are in essence homeless and penniless. If you can explain why it would make any sense whatsoever to continue to take on guardianship of this helpless life, by all means share."

Dickerson looked silently at the baby cradled in his left arm, sucking sleepily on a pacifier. He shook his head, "I know you're right, Pastor. I just don't want to give her up. She's all I have." His eyes glistened with tears when he looked up then, "Did these people say they take babies with, you know, problems?"

"I didn't ask. But I will. Tomorrow when I call her back, with your permission."

"And she'd go to a different state? And have a family?"

"Yes, that's what the woman said."

"Then I guess it's the best thing. I want to be there when they, um, take her."

"I understand. We'll go together."

The next morning after he'd spoken with the

63

representative, Reverend Phillips reported the good news. They would surrender the baby that afternoon. She'd be in a new home within twenty-four hours, far away from Armani, and Miss Crazy.

And, sadly, far away from Dickerson.

They met in a nondescript storefront in a strip mall. It smelled of fresh paint and the furnishings looked new. They were simple—office chairs, a potted plant, a desk with a computer and printer on it. "Excuse the appearance. It must look like we are a freshman company. Actually, this is our newest office and we are just getting everything moved in. Please sit down." Reverend Phillips and Dickerson sat across from her desk. She walked around to the car seat Dickerson had placed protectively next to his chair and looked inside with a grandmotherly expression, though she couldn't have been over thirty years old. "Oh, how sweet. And you say she has some sort of disability?"

"Yes, ma'am. She don't have no arms. But she's perfect in every other way," Dickerson quickly added.

"I'm sure she is. And I think I have just the people who will want to take her." She smiled and sat down opposite them. "Now, the paperwork is actually quite minimal since you don't have any background information on her. Where did you say you found her?"

"I didn't. Suffice it to say she wasn't wanted and I been taking care of her."

"Certainly. Now are you ready to sign these papers,

Mr. — ?"

Reverend Phillips interrupted, "I'll be acting as legal representative for the baby since she is part of my congregation. I'll sign." He signed the forms she handed across the desk. The men stood up. The reverend shook her hand with a smile, "Thank you. This is providence, to be sure, having met you when we did."

Dickerson bent down and unstrapped the sleeping newborn from her seat. He held her close and whispered, "I guess this is it, sugar. I'm sure glad I got to meet you. That kid in the cowboy hat was right. You sure are something special." He leaned down and kissed her, then, a tear dropping on her cheek.

Stepping toward Ms. Frances, he didn't see the trash can his foot kicked until he heard the hollow thud. Halting mid-apology when he saw what lay in the bottom, he suddenly jerked around and hollered at the reverend, "Get the seat, and get out now!" and ran out the door with the baby. Phillips had no choice but to follow.

They drove back to the safe room at breakneck speed, the reverend demanding an explanation. Dickerson just repeated, "I knew it didn't feel right." Infuriated and confused, the reverend followed him into the bedroom where Lola was sitting in bed, staring into space.

Dickerson started packing the baby's things into a bag. "I gotta get her outta here. I gotta keep her safe."

The reverend stepped in front of Dickerson and demanded an answer. "What's gotten into you, man? What did you see at One For All?"

"It was in the bottom. I saw it in the bottom of the

trash can. Had a man and woman half-naked in EXTRA LARGE PRINT."

The reverend had no idea what he was talking about, "I'm going to have to call the police."

"Don't you dare!" Dickerson was yelling now. He'd never thrown a punch at a clergyman, but he would do whatever he had to to protect this baby.

"O...F...A...!!!" Lola screamed the letters.

Both men turned in shock at the first sounds she'd uttered in over a week.

"O...F...A..." she repeated dismally. "It was on Frank's badge. One For All is OFA. He knows them, knew them, as Overseas Franchise Administration. OFA." She was crying now.

Convinced, Reverend began helping Dickerson pack. "You have to get out of here right away. They could be here any minute. They must have traced Lola's call and set up the phony chance appointment in order to lure the baby out into the open. Listen, I went to the apartment and you were right, everything was trashed. But the boxes were there in the closet, just like you said they'd be. I brought them back here to the safe room and put their contents in this army bag here. I know a place up north you can go to. I'm sorry I can't do more."

"You've done so much already, pastor. Thank you." Dickerson embraced the man. He picked up the car seat holding the baby, put the diaper bag over his shoulder and began to walk toward the door.

"Wait. I'm coming with," Lola jumped out of bed, fully clothed, including her shoes and coat underneath the blankets. The men stared, shocked. "What? I had a feeling. Listen, I have a car and I've got no reason to stay here now that Frank is...now that Frank's not coming home. I can help you with her."

It had been two weeks since she'd lost Frank. Grief had swallowed her whole until a tiny tickle of a thought had worked its way out. She grabbed hold of it, her escape from the acid filled abyss that ate at her day and night. It grew into a driving force that expelled her forcefully onto the outside of the pain. She relished the relief and purpose this control gave her, and she fed it with fantasy, planning and determination—for revenge.

They smiled gratefully and the reverend grabbed her duffel bag for her. It was lying next to the door, clothes inside, her loaded revolver rolled neatly inside a sweatshirt.

CHAPTER FOUR

# The Carpet Bag

The room was large enough for screams to echo. There was a bed with tight straps on it. He was naked. That was all he could piece together in the disorienting black reality that was now his existence. He had no sense of time—only the gnawing hunger pangs told him it may have been morning, then noon, then dinnertime that first day. The second day they, too, were indistinguishable. He really had no idea how many days had passed. His hoarse voice squeaked out the anguish he felt as he lay in his own excrement and urine. The room wasn't large enough for its pungent smell to escape his scorched nostrils.

Eventually, the door opened. He heard the lock turn and then a light blinded his eyes as it spilled in from the hallway. He squeezed them tightly together as blue dots danced and a searing pain cut through his head. A switch was flipped up, the door was shut and footsteps clicked across the tile floor. "Look at me." It was a familiar voice from the past, the recent past, maybe, but still long, long ago.

He kept his eyes closed, afraid of the light. The blow took him by surprise. The impact of the hand across his left cheek forced his head to the right. He froze his neck this way, a futile attempt to avoid further abuse. Terrified when he opened his eyes and still saw nothing, relieved when the solid blackness dissolved into a wispy gray and then a soft golden glow entered his periphery, he focused. He tried to do as the man said, to look at him, but when he turned his head, the man was not in view.

"Let's get to work, shall we?" the man's voice came from behind the bed. He came around the side and stated, "It's time for you to give us what we need."

"What do you need?"

"Answers."

"I don't have answers. And you'd just kill me after I gave them to you if I did."

"Wrong. You do have answers," the man smiled. "You haven't even heard the questions yet, silly boy."

"I have questions of my own."

"I'm sure you do. I will be happy to answer them all for you," his words confirmed their intent to dispose of him regardless. "Do you like games? How about we toss a coin to see who talks first? If it's heads I will answer one question for you. If tails, you start."

"I don't like games."

This slap knocked his right cheek to the left with a hollow smacking sound. "Yet you will play. Because you have questions of your own." He pulled out a quarter and spun it high into the air before catching it in his other hand and slapping it down flat on the back of his hand. "Heads. Fire away."

"Where is she?"

This question seemed to surprise the man. He shook his head a little, "That was going to be my question. Who are you talking about?"

"You know. What did you do with her?"

"Now you are just trying to be clever. Let me reverse the same question to you. What did *you* do with *her*?"

"I don't know who you are talking about, either. I didn't do anything with her."

"I can see we are getting nowhere with our little game here, so let's try a different approach, shall we?" The man snapped latex gloves on, held up a small alligator clip attached to a red wire and another with a black one. At the end of the bed he pinched them onto both big toes and excitedly lifted a hand crank generator from an old telephone as if trying to get approval from the imprisoned man. Receiving none, he went on. "Primitive, I know. But if you knew what I was sparing you from, you'd have gotten this conversation over with and told me where she was. Oh well." He gleefully turned the handle, sending electricity jolting through the man's body.

The man went into uncontrollable spasms, then. Clenching his teeth together to avoid biting off his own tongue, he screamed through them as he flailed. His limbs worked involuntarily against the cloth straps that bound him, rubbing until bloody. His heart felt as if it were exploding with the pressure in his chest, his lungs went on overload, gasping in spurts of air through heaving nostrils. A hum intensified in his ears as his eardrums were stimulated until he was sure they'd pop with the force. And he smelled it before he felt it, the acrid burning of soiled linens against his nude flesh, his wet groin area conducting heat. The last horrible thought he had before passing out was that it wasn't just the sheets that were on fire, it was him.

When he came to it could have been days or even weeks later, he had no way of knowing. His skin felt raw but he could tell he'd been cleaned up, his wounds dressed and crisp, new bedding enveloped him. He was still naked, still tied down, with an IV line stuck in his left wrist, pulled taught out to a hook on a metal stand out of his reach. He saw all of this clearly by the soft light of the lamp behind him and was grateful for it. He supposed they were keeping him alive until they could get information out of him. He supposed the kinder gentler treatment was part of a new tactic. He supposed giving them answers would lead to others being hurt. He decided that the only information he had, namely what the business card he'd slipped into Dickerson's pocket had read, would go to the grave with him. Not that it really mattered; Dickerson and the baby were gone into the cold abyss of a long-forgotten quarry lake. Lola was gone, too. But she loved that church and he would protect it with what remained of his life. Her name involuntarily escaped his lips. "Lola."

"You'll never see her again, Frank. You might as well give us what we're looking for. We're going to get it out of you one way or another," a raspy female voice startled him. He placed it, even through his drugged, exhausted mind and though he'd mainly been grunted at by her in passing. The chair she was sitting on creaked as she rose from it. She walked around to where he could see her, placing her paperback in the heavy satchel he'd never seen her without. He'd heard rumors about what lay inside. Raw fear pierced his bravado. He stiffened, staring at it.

"What, you afraid of this little old thing?" she laughed and rummaged around for a moment. Pulling out a black box, she set it on his chest. It was lightweight, but Frank's chest felt heavy with it nonetheless. She opened up the lid, pulled down the front toward his neck and folded open two sides. Focusing on it was difficult because of the proximity to his face, but Frank ascertained electronic gauges, knobs and dials, none of which he could decipher the meaning of. She seemed proud to show him the contraption. "We have access to the most modern technology because of our international success. It is imperative that those who work with us maintain the highest level of security and loyalty, and most do. As you know, we pay well and ask little in return. Each job given to our employees is specialized and specific. There is rarely a need for those on our payroll to have to step outside of the box, excuse the pun I suppose. However, every once in a while, we unfortunately ask for more than a person is able or willing to perform, and then we are left tying up loose ends. I'm sure you understand."

She pulled out something from a small drawer on the

back of the black box and placed an earpiece into Frank's left ear.

"We have some loose ends which plague us regarding recent events. Namely, why our diver was unable to retrieve bodies from the bottom of the pond?" Frank's heart first soared at the thought that Dickerson may have escaped with the baby, then plummeted with the realization that they may have led the company right to Lola's church.

"Where could they have gone? We know he did not return to his apartment or mother. We found no evidence of them having been at your house. Which leads us to two glaring questions. Where is she?"

"Where is who? The baby? I don't know!" Frank burst out.

"No, Frank, where is your wife?" His head spun then with the new idea that she may still be alive, hiding somewhere, perhaps helping rescue that baby.

She slid another earpiece into his right ear. "I will give you one more chance to cooperate, Frank. As you know, practically every square inch of our parking garage is monitored by camera. We know you saw it was a baby in that trunk, we know you pushed out the seat for it. What we haven't been able to figure out is what you slid into Dickerson's pocket in passing. Now, we will find your wife, and your only hope for a happy reunion is for you to just answer this one tiny little question: What did the little white card say?"

"You're lying! You'll never let me live. I'll never tell you anything." Every cell in his body ached with the desire to be with her again, yet his resolve to protect her was strengthened immeasurably by the hope of her survival.

"Very well then. Let's begin, shall we?" she didn't try to hide the glee in her voice. "Nurse!" The young woman must have been standing outside the door, because she rushed right in. "Meet Frank. He is no longer considered a loyal employee. Did you put the serum into the IV as ordered?"

"Yes, ma'am," she nodded while glancing at Frank. "I took into account his height, weight and age, then prepared exactly the amount to get the results you require."

"Fine, then." She began to mutter as she leaned in close to the black box, squinting at the numbers on it before turning a knob right and another left. Bulbs lit up and it hummed as it warmed up. "I used to do all of it myself, you know. Didn't need all these employees and their incompetence. Didn't need someone driving me places or measuring out drugs. Didn't need security, for that matter. But our organization got stronger and my damn eyesight got weaker and here we are, aren't we? Just one big happy family."

She turned on the nurse then. "You're lucky I value your loyalty over your stupidity. If you'd told me when that mistake was birthed that it was a freak of nature we could have disposed of it right then and there like we did her mother."

"Ma'am, respectfully, I tried to tell you..."

"Ma'am, I tried to tell you," she mimicked in a sing-song voice. "Shut up and get out of here until I call you again, you stupid little bitch!"

Frank watched her walk out, thinking that if she'd had

a tail it would have been firmly tucked between her legs.

The Bag Lady lifted a toggle switch and the humming sound grew louder. Then Frank felt himself going down into a relaxed sleepy dream of remembering.

⤳

It was last week. The Suit had dropped him off at his car and he had driven home at breakneck speed after work to be with Lola. Pulling into the driveway, he'd rushed into the house and heard only silence. He'd called for her, "Lola! Are you home darling?" He'd begun a frantic search through the house then, calling for her, peering hopefully through each door he flung open. Where could she be? She was always home. Except for when she was at church. That was it, wasn't it? She must have been at a women's meeting. Didn't she go to those? A key rattled in the door and she'd entered, breathless, carrying a bag of groceries. He walked to her, relieved, and pulled her into an embrace. The food tumbled out of her grasp, crashed and rolled around the floor.

She laughed, "Well it's nice to see you, too, dear!" and bent down to pick up the mess.

"Leave it," he said, but she ignored him and kept scooping things back into the brown bag. "I said leave it, Lola!" his voice became louder. He didn't know why, but suddenly he kicked her, hard, in the stomach.

Her body jack-knifed in confusion and pain. "Frank, what's gotten into you?" she croaked out.

"You need to be loyal. That's the most important thing,

you know." He was on top of her now, straddling her with his hands around her neck. He pushed his thumbs into her throat and spat out the words, "Loyal to me, not to that damn Sparta Baptist Church!"

Her eyes, full of betrayal and confusion, pleaded for him to let go. But he didn't. Not until the pulse on the other side of his thumbs sped up erratically, weakened, slowed and stopped.

He rolled off of her onto the cluttered floor and fell asleep, satisfied that she was safe now. He'd never lose her again.

When Frank awoke he was sobbing uncontrollably, guilt and shame sucker punched him in the stomach but the straps held him back from folding into a fetal position. He'd killed her. He remembered now. Every detail was etched clearly in his mind. He knew the Suit had drugged him somehow, knew that he hadn't been in his right mind, but he also knew with complete certainty that he had murdered his beloved wife. As far as he was concerned, they couldn't kill him soon enough.

Carpet Bagger packed up her little box with a satisfied smirk on her face. She put the earpieces carefully into the little drawer, placed the entire contraption into her big bag and stood looking at Frank for a moment. "Sparta Baptist Church. Thank you, Frank. You've been very helpful to us after all. We'll send our representative there first thing tomorrow morning to offer our services." She called the nurse back in and told her, "You know how to wrap things up in here," and left.

The nurse unhooked the IV from Frank's arm and looked sadly at him as he muttered, "Lola, Lola, Lola" over and over, eyes glazed, drooling, still caught up in his dark memory.

She whispered, "Listen, mister. I know you tried to save that pretty little baby. I called, you know, and tried to warn your wife that you were in trouble. I shouldn't have meddled at all. I'm stuck, you know. Stuck in this job like you were. I thought I could do something good for a change. I'm gonna give you a second chance to go warn them before the company finds them." She injected a two-inch needle into his bicep and pushed the stopper down a third of the way.

"Lola." He repeated dumbly. Maybe he could still save her. Maybe she was still at the house, sleeping on the floor. He'd help her put the groceries away.

The nurse carefully hid the syringe under his left hand. She'd injected an amount of venom that would slow his breathing and pulse to imperceptible levels. She'd left enough in the syringe to put down a horse.

Twenty minutes later a very dead appearing man was wheeled down to the furnace room below the labor and delivery suite on the bottom floor of the warehouse. "Good luck," she breathed as she left him parked there for the head of security to push onto the conveyer that evening. The furnace was never fired until after midnight in order to keep suspicion down regarding the smoke that poured out of the building. That way it dissipated in the dark night air, and no one was the wiser.

The nurse went home and swallowed a bottle of sleeping pills. She slept better than she had in years.

~*~

The head of security brought a box of Frank's things with him when he came downstairs. He set it on the hospital bed, "Howdy, Frankie! How do you like being dead? Not talking? Well, that's nothing new, is it?" He laughed. "Thought you might want your stuff back. Hope you're not mad at me about last week. I was just doing my job, you understand."

He walked over to the furnace and pushed a few buttons. A fire sputtered to life on the other side of the glass door. "Gonna take a little while to heat up in there. That gives us a chance to talk a little more, what do you say? Want to play a game? Oh, that's right, you don't like games. Well, what do you like? Let's take a look in this here box, shall we?"

He wheeled a stool to the bed's side and began rummaging. Producing a holstered pistol he exclaimed, "You got good taste in guns, Frankie. I've always been a nine-millimeter guy myself. Can I have it for my collection? What's that? Traceable? You're right, of course. It's gonna go in the fire."

He dug around some more, muttering, "Clothes, a belt. Gosh, looks like we got your entire issued security guard uniform here. Don't worry, no one will ever know you were here and failed so miserably at assassinating our boss.

You weren't real sneaky, Frankie, even you gotta admit that. Parking out in front of the building in your flashy car all night. Tsk, tsk, tsk. Oh yeah, I wanted to make sure you knew where it is now. Remember that quarry Dickerson found? Apparently it's pretty deep. It will serve us well when we have things we need to make disappear, you know, things that won't fit into the furnace here."

"Look what we have here!" He pulled out Frank's wallet and stuffed the cash within into his pocket. "You don't mind, do you?" Then he pulled out a picture of Lola and whistled. "She's a looker, Frank. You're a lucky man. I can see why you wanted to protect her. She's not really my type, though." He tossed the wallet and photo into the box and then moved in right next to Frank's right ear. "I like 'em young, Frankie. Real young. Most men who utilize our company do. But I guess you don't know anything about all that, Mr. Door Security Man. You weren't even a cog in the wheel of this machine we're involved in here. Insignificant and worthless." He stood up then and went to the furnace and threw the box in. He walked around the bed, cutting the bindings off of Frank's legs and arms.

"It's a shame, really, that the boss didn't think she'd be marketable without those arms. People got strange fetishes, you know." He leaned down and put his face near Frank's, whispering, "I'd like to show you mine." He bent closer to put his lips on Frank's. Frank suddenly sat up and in a fluid motion stabbed the hidden needle deep into the man's neck. Shock widened his eyes, the venom blackened them, and he slumped to the ground.

Frank worked quickly. He borrowed the dead man's

clothes, lifted him onto the conveyor and fed the body into the fire along with his hospital clothing. No one raised an eyebrow at seeing the head of security walk briskly out of the building.

He really wasn't sure where he was going until he arrived there. He stood in the kitchen of his destroyed home and it all flooded back again, the nightmare that had happened here. His arrival home, her bringing in groceries, his strangling her to death. There was the evidence, food lay all over the floor, rotting. He picked it all up and put it into the cupboards and fridge. She must have gone to get more. She was such a good, loyal wife. "Lola," he smiled and went out into the night. He would find her. He would help her put away the groceries. He would take her out for ice cream. He would find her if it took him the rest of his life.

It almost did.

# PART TWO

## FLASH FORWARD

## CHAPTER FIVE

# The Hermit House

Scott's Pine citizens kept to themselves not because they were unfriendly, but because they were incredibly busy. Theirs was a commuter community since industry had dried up in the last thirty years. Folks and their folks had settled and established a town two-hundred years ago when three enterprising young men had picked this spot in Clayburne County to build their brainchild, the Parlin Paper Company. Natural resources were plentiful in this high forest area. The town grew as the workforce of lumber jacks, lumber mills, restaurants, supply stores, and paper salesmen grew. They were stragglers who'd become close knit families and friends, stubbornly remaining that way despite the economic fallout when Parlin Paper went bankrupt, succumbing to the electronic age.

They traveled the two hour drive each day to the nearest city, began working from home, and kept the town's jobs filled. The school, a bakery, a grocery store, the hospital and barber shop were saturated with "old families." Parlins, Howsens, and McNabs were the main names. Most people were less than four times removed from one of these, and proud of it. They were the original town founders, their names graced street signs and business signs. Theirs were the tallest monuments in the cemetery.

In a town like this, outsiders were rare. Those who'd tried to settle here were often enamored by the idyllic appearance of the town, the atmosphere created by a people who kept their streets, sidewalks and storefronts in pristine shape. Maintained decorative details titillated even the subconscious eye and people were drawn immediately to the idea of homesteading here.

Those wanting an isolated lifestyle passed through to other housing markets after viewing this facade. Those wanting social connection and belonging moved on after a few months of living in a place where they soon realized they'd never be accepted, would always be considered outsiders.

This reality suited a hermit just fine. The one who lived in the house on McNab Hill had never left it since moving in almost 20 years ago. Folks knew he lived there. He'd bought the place after the latest outsiders had vacated. It had run through a string of new owners since Marty McNab's greedy nephew had put it on the market following his uncle's death. The old man who'd taken residence never came into town, had a housekeeper who got his mail, groceries and necessities each week, and answered curious questions politely while guarding his privacy. That's why folks knew she lived there with him, in the carriage house.

That's how they knew he was alone up there. That's how they knew he was a harmless older man who just wanted to keep to himself. This suited Scott's Pine just fine.

The housekeeper only came to town for three reasons — to get what she needed for her employer, to go to the library and to go to church. She came to Sunday service, sat in the back row and kept to herself. The pastor had tried to go beyond small talk but she'd never offered more.

The librarian knew her as a voracious reader. She'd sit and read the papers, especially those published in the capital city, and check out armloads of books. She had eclectic tastes, too. For a while the rumor was that she or the hermit was a children's book author because that's what she checked out. But after that phase there was no rhyme or reason to her selections. History, science, teenage fiction, bestsellers, puzzle books, graphic novels, how-to manuals, medical books—all were checked out under the name Sarah Stone.

The storekeeper, Mr. Howsen, received an order each Monday, filled it throughout the week and helped Sarah load it into the trunk of her old car each Friday afternoon. Most items were standard—bread, milk, eggs and rice. Sometimes when she came in she picked out sewing notions and material, but he never saw her wearing the clothing she'd made. He sometimes chuckled at the idea of the hermit in the pink satin she'd bought, but assumed she was selling these things online or sending them to a loved one somewhere else, maybe a granddaughter or niece. But he'd never asked. His wife was constantly reminding him that he really should mind his own business; after all, he was just a simple storekeeper in a simple town now. All that really concerned him was the sizeable bill the hermit ran up each month and paid promptly with crisp new hundred dollar bills. Still, he sometimes wondered as she drove away just what was really going on up in that hermit house high on the hill.

⌒ℳ⌒

She stood in front of the full length mirror and turned in the dress slowly. This was Sarah's finest work yet and the girl was grateful, but no matter how hard she tried she couldn't ignore the fact that something was horribly wrong. Still. No matter how pretty she was wrapped up, she was ugly, imperfect, incomplete. She hated her appearance. But she loved Sarah, so she forced a smile and turned to thank her. Sarah pulled her into a hug and whispered, "You're beautiful, Ann."

"I love the dress. Thank you, Sarah! I want to go show Father." She ran to the living room where her father was sitting in his ancient recliner, reading a book, jazz playing softly on the stereo in the corner. He looked up and smiled. Setting his book down on a table, he gestured for her to come sit on his lap. "Father, you know I'm too big for that now." Their game began.

"No, never, Annie. You will always be my little lump of sugar."

"More like giant lump!"

He chuckled as she sat carefully beside him in his chair. He held an arm around her and whispered, "You are beautiful, Ann."

"I love you, Father. Thank you for the dress. It is a perfect birthday present."

"You are so welcome. Our Sarah has outdone herself with the meal she has prepared for us, as well as this gorgeous dress. You deserve every bit of it. I can't believe it's been nineteen years since I first picked you up and held you close to me."

"Will you tell me the story now that I am nineteen?"

"Oh, yes, I suppose I will. But not tonight. Tonight is a night for celebration and not reflection!" This was his standard answer and her standard response was to allow him to change the subject. This time she pushed. "Father, will you tell me tomorrow, then? All of it? Promise!"

A shadow crossed his wrinkled face but he promised, "Yes, darling. It's time you knew it all. I will tell you tomorrow."

It had taken almost two decades but he finally saw movement in this old church. It had originally been founded with social justice of paramount concern, and had gone through many phases in its history. It was built when the Underground Railroad was still being used and the hidden cellar deep below the basement had temporarily housed a few escaping slaves. The civic minded parson who ran the church in those days kept no official records, but his personal diary had been found buried within the walls of the church when they'd renovated the sanctuary a number of years ago. Now it sat in the library for the proud perusal of congregants.

The Great Depression necessitated outreach to the hungry and needy, and church members were not immune. They brought their food together and made enormous pots of soup, which they ladled out gratefully to each other and to their neighbors.

During World War II the church became a place of funerals, social groups of grieving and praying women, and a center of action for the war effort. It was a center for organizing recycling and scrap drives in the nearby neighborhoods. Volunteers worked with after-school programs for children whose fathers were at war, and mothers forced into the workplace.

The church fell asleep sometime after that. More and more government agencies were developed to meet the needs of the poor and needy, and families became more self-sufficient. Organized religion left an increasingly bad taste in people's mouths as leaders fell in disgrace, the separation of church and state was touted, and its views deemed antiquated and unscientific in a postmodern thinking society.

The Cold War saw a fearful nation become introverted and paranoid. The church turned the lower chambers into an underground bunker that would help a few survive nuclear fallout—the few who'd invested the most money into the church, presumably. Attempts from that point on to revive the social conscience of the church had failed miserably. People were just too busy or apathetic or politically correct to get involved.

That changed for Sparta Baptist not because Reverend Phillips was hired, not because he wanted it, not because of his phenomenal preaching, but because of an unlikely event that happened fifteen years almost to the day of Dickerson and Lola's escape. God showed up.

It was during the offering of all things. People were writing checks, digging into pockets, stifling yawns and doodling on their bulletins. Standard procedure would be to have the prayer and dismissal after the plates had made their rounds. But when the ushers handed the four metal plates to the four people in the first four rows across the front of the sanctuary, every one of these people pulled their hands back as if they'd been electrocuted and the plates clattered to the floor noisily. Everyone who hadn't seen what happened heard what came next. A woman who'd come in off the streets and was sitting in the back stood up and yelled, "This is the kind of fasting I have chosen: Loosen the chains of wickedness, untie the straps of the slaves, let the oppressed go free, and break every yoke!" Then she sat back down in the wheelchair she'd been confined to for the past fifteen years.

A thick silence permeated the room for many shocked minutes. Then first one, then another person announced joyfully:

"Hey, I can hear from my left ear!"

"I can move my neck without pain!"

"I think my leg just grew out to match my other leg!"

"My ulcer isn't hurting anymore!"

And blind Mr. Fredricks, who gave candy to all the children who found him before the service, stood in the middle of the room, tears running down his face. "I can see! I can see all of you!" Overcome, he began running around the sanctuary, throwing candy. Tootsie Rolls rained down on giggling adults.

The healed and hopeful worshiped and talked for hours. The church had been awakened.

The woman who no longer needed her wheelchair walked into Reverend Phillip's office the next day and pitched her idea of serving meals to those who were facing homelessness. Her name was Tara, she said, and she'd be happy to head things up.

They began that afternoon. The people in the sanctuary who were still worshiping and praying joined in making sandwiches and inviting people in. Sparta Baptist members boldly prayed for their guests. Some were healed, all were touched and encouraged. Word spread quickly about the miraculous Sunday service they'd had and the outpouring of God's Spirit that was happening still as people laid hands on the sick and broken.

Into this setting a few years later came a man who had clearly been alone for a long long time. He said he was a friend of Tara's. His eyes confused, receding oily hair standing on end, clothes filthy with the grime of the bridge he'd been sleeping under. He sat silently, devoured a bowl of stew and stuffed a piece of bread into his pocket for later. When he stood to leave a volunteer asked him if she could pray for him. "Unnn," he grunted past her and walked out the door.

He came back two weeks later, then one. He would have remained unnoticed in the crowd of body odor and poverty if he hadn't seen her that day. He'd eaten his fill and was ready to get back to the little cat he fed his bread to when he passed her in the hallway. "Lola!" he suddenly grabbed her shoulders and pushed her against the wall. He wasn't trying to hurt her, but she startled and screamed for help. Two men came running, grabbed his hands to pull him off of her. He turned around swinging. He wouldn't let them hurt her! "Lola! Lola! I'll protect you!" His fist landed on an older man's jaw before three other men had him held tight.

"I'll call the police, Reverend Phillips," the shaken up woman said.

"There's no need. I know who this is," he rubbed his sore chin and asked the men who were restraining Frank to bring him down to the safe room.

Sarah laughed as she dished eggs onto two plates. Ann was at it again, attempting to coax her father into getting another pet. Verbally he wasn't budging, but there was a twinkle in his eye. He was as big a pet lover as she was and all three of them knew where this conversation would end. She would get another cat, or fish, or frog or hamster. She would promise to take care of it and he would let her. But for now the argument raged on.

"Tell me, daughter, how many cats does one girl need, really?"

"It's more a question of how many cats need me, Father. I was on the humane society website and I saw a video of one who was practically asking for me by name."

"It was just yawning, dear." he teased.

She shot him a fake exasperated look and went on, "She has white and brown markings and the longest, softest fur I've ever seen."

"So, you touched it through the computer? Amazing what technology can do these days!" he smirked.

"You know what I meant. If it's still there Friday can Sarah go get it for us?"

"Us? How did I get included in this scheme? Absolutely not! I forbid it!" his voice was mock horror.

"Oh, thank you, Father! She kissed him on the cheek, then looked seriously into his eyes. "And our conversation? You promised it would be today."

"Yes, darling. I haven't forgotten. Let's have a coffee date in my study this afternoon after my nap. That will give you a chance to finish your studies and that way we won't be interrupted. Except perhaps by a cat or two?"

She laughed. The truth was they didn't have even one cat at the moment, but her father liked to pretend the house was overrun with them, "Okay, then. It's a date." She left the room smiling.

Sarah sat across from him and they were silent for a few minutes. "That's not going to be an easy conversation."

"I don't even know where to start. You'll join us, won't you?"

"Yes, of course. I am part of her story, too."

"You certainly are, Lola. You've been a wonderful mother to her and friend to me. Thank God for saving her. Our Ann is indeed something special."

"Dickerson, it has been my privilege." They both smiled at the first use of their real names in almost two decades.

He reached across the table and grabbed her hand. "Can we pray together for her? And for this afternoon?"

"Of course, God's seen us through so much over the years. He'll see us through whatever comes next."

"I'm afraid she'll leave us, Lola, er, Sarah."

"Me, too. She is tired of being stuck in this house and curious about the outside world. But they'd destroy her. I don't just mean OFA. I mean people, society. We've protected and enabled her to do so many things a normal child can do. But she isn't, and they will make it all too clear. No one will love her the way we have."

"Let's pray for that, too, then. She's in God's hands, not ours."

"You're right," she bowed her head with him.

Frank remained calm only when they brought in the volunteer he'd mistaken for Lola to sit across the table from him. Reverend Phillips asked him questions and tried to make sense of his answers, piecing together the last nineteen years of the man's life. He opened up to "Lola."

He told her about how he'd been looking for her all these years, wandering around the entire country. He'd found odd jobs to get by, slept under bridges or in shelters and stopped at every grocery store and supermarket he'd passed. He'd returned every few months to the city and home they'd shared.

Staring at her quizzically, he asked, "Where did you go? After I killed you? I couldn't find you. I went to the grocery store but you weren't there. I went back to the house but it was cleaned up, then there was a for sale sign outside, then the locks were different and other people moved in. Where were you, Lola?"

The volunteer looked at the Reverend for guidance. He nodded for her to continue to play along and said, "Frank, you didn't kill Lola. She's alive and well. You love her."

"Yes, I did. I remember it all." He lay his head on his arms and sobbed then. "Lola, can you ever forgive me? I'm so sorry. I didn't mean to do it. I wasn't myself."

The young woman comforted him, "Yes, of course, Frank. It's okay."

He looked up, relieved. "I'm just glad I found you. I'll protect you now. I'll protect you."

Pastor Phillips asked, "Frank, why didn't you come directly here to Sparta Baptist looking for Lola?"

"I don't know. Is that what this church is called? Should I have remembered that name from somewhere?"

"Do you remember the little white card you slipped into Dickerson's pocket?"

"Yes, but I couldn't recall what was on it. My memory of that time is sketchy at best, I'm afraid."

"Frank, would you like to stay here for a few days in the safe room and rest? It will give us a chance to sort out some things. I think I can help you piece together the puzzle of your past a bit, and I'm sure Lola has many questions for you, too."

"I guess so. But only if I can bring Millie."

"Um, who's Millie? Your girlfriend?"

"No!" he vehemently reassured everyone, "I haven't been with anyone, Lola. I've been looking for you. I've been real lonely but I just kept looking for you."

"So, Millie is...?"

"Millie's my cat." They all laughed.

Sarah pulled the fresh baked brownies out of the oven and set them on the counter to cool before cutting them. Coffee was brewing, its aroma spreading from the kitchen down the hallway and into Ann's bedroom. She came bounding in a few minutes later. "Need help?"

Sarah found some way to say yes and mean it every time Ann asked. She had always been purposeful about pointing out what Ann could do instead of the countless things she couldn't. "Yes, I'm glad you finally got your nose out of that book. Can you please go wake up the sleepy old bear and I'll meet you both in the study."

"Sure, wish me luck!"

"Just stay out of range and you should be fine." Ann's father had a habit of pretending to be asleep until she'd gotten right up close to him, then grabbing her in a surprise bear hug. She loved the games he played with her.

He was facing away from her, folded in the large quilt Sarah had made for his seventieth birthday. She called playfully from the doorway, "Time to come out from hibernation!"

He didn't stir. The game was on.

Ann stomped two steps closer and cleared her throat loudly. Nothing. Then she crept right up to the side of the bed silently, hoping to surprise him. She leaned in close to his ear and loudly exclaimed, "You missed me!" before jumping back out of his reach, expecting him to turn and make a grab for her. He didn't.

Confusion lifted her left eyebrow as she tried again, "Father? Are you awake? This isn't funny anymore." Concerned, she walked to the other side of his bed and looked hard at him. He was a statue, a great big beloved statue, frozen inside a brightly colored blanket. His eyes wide open, unblinking. She ran from the room then, screaming for Sarah, crashing into her as the two met in the hallway. Slumped on the floor, she watched the older woman scurry into the bedroom.

Sarah returned minutes later, weeping, and confirmed what Ann already knew. Her father had fallen into a deeper sleep than she would ever be able to rouse him from. Their games were over.

The funeral was, of course, a private affair. Sarah dug the hole herself under his favorite tree. Pulling him into position for burial had been an unsavory business consisting of pushing, pulling and rolling him off of the bed and into a rough box she'd made of pine boards she'd pulled off the side of an old shed. She'd put large casters on the bottom and wheeled it with some difficulty out to the backyard. Then she'd rolled it carefully down into the grave site. It would have been easier if Ann had been able to help. She could have pulled with a rope wrapped around her waist while Sarah pushed, but she knew it was better to spare the poor girl the added grief.

They played his favorite jazz piece, Coltrane's *A Love Supreme*, told him how much they loved him, and Sarah read a passage from the Bible, Psalm 23. The wooden marker Sarah pushed in place after throwing in the last shovelful of dirt read simply, "Here lies a good, good man. He will be missed."

The two of them became inseparable. Ann inconsolable, Sarah worked hard to fill an impossible gap. She mostly just held her, smoothed her hair, coaxed her into eating enough to sustain her, and prayed.

Days grew into weeks, weeks into months, and Ann began to come out of the dependent, protective cocoon she'd encased herself in upon losing her father. She had been changed, not into a butterfly, but a sullen, silent, sad young woman.

Sarah never got phone calls. She made them, but never received them, especially since Dickerson wasn't there to call when she was in town to ask her to pick up one more thing he'd thought of in her absence. She'd all but forgotten what her ringtone sounded like and jumped out of her skin when she heard it rattling in her purse. It was evening, she'd said goodnight to Ann, gone to her little apartment to watch TV before turning in herself. It had only been a couple weeks since Ann had felt comfortable sleeping in the house alone.

She dug out her phone and glanced at the number. It wasn't familiar, but how could it be? No one called her. No one outside of Scott's Pine even had her number. Assuming it was a wrong number or sales call, she shut off her phone and went to bed.

The next day was Friday and she needed to go get supplies in town. Flipping her phone on to call and make sure her order was ready before driving the five miles in, she was surprised to hear no less than thirty notification chimes. "What?" They were all from the same number as the night before. They left no voice mails. Annoyed, she called the number, ready to give a piece of her mind.

It rang four times before he picked up. "Hello? Lola?"

She sat down hard in her kitchen chair, breathless upon hearing the voice from her past. "Yes, Reverend, it's me. Um, how are you?" She wasn't sure what to say.

"Fine, fine. Are you sitting down, Lola?"

"Yes."

"I have someone here who wants to speak with you. And you are sitting down?"

She laughed a little, "Yes, yes, I'm sitting down."

"Okay, here you go," she heard him pass the phone to someone else.

"Lola?"

Now the room spun out of control. The phone fell and she remembered, crazily, the last time she'd dropped a phone, twenty years ago, when a different voice had told her that Frank had been terminated. But now it was him, this voice on this falling phone, and she landed with a thud right beside it.

## CHAPTER SIX

# The Strangers in Town

The gist of the conversation they had over the next few days was, "I can't explain it all right now, Ann dear. But I have to go to the capital to take care of something. I'm not sure how long I'll be gone. It shouldn't be more than a couple of weeks. Your clothes are all clean and put away, I've filled the freezer with food for you and I know you'll be okay. Are you sure you won't come with me?" Ann shook her head. Sarah hated to see her this way, hated the thought of leaving her even more, but this was what Ann was choosing. She knew that for a girl who'd barely left her home in nineteen years, a trip so far outside of her comfort zone was both an exhilarating and terrifying thought. In her current grief-ridden state, terror won.

Yet, Sarah's offers to postpone the trip any longer were met with Ann's reassurance. "I'll be fine, really." They were a few words of a precious handful Ann had spoken since losing her father, and Sarah believed them. She had no choice, really.

So Sarah left to go to her long lost husband and Ann found herself, for the first time in her young life, thoroughly, completely, achingly alone. She was surprisingly independent for someone with such a glaringly limiting birth defect. This was testament to how her father and Sarah had raised her. They'd cheered her on at every attempt at trying something new, and reassured her at every setback that there was a way to modify circumstances to ensure future successes. They made her home as accessible as possible through ordering specialized equipment and use of their own creative invention. Dickerson had a keen eye for how to simplify tasks. Sarah and he also lived at her ability level, doing things the way she did, using some of the same resources available to her. It was commonplace, for instance, for all three to eat their food without forks, by putting their mouths to their plates. Hygiene was completed by stepping on a series of buttons in the shower that activated water, shampoo or soap on brushes set into one wall, and even toothpaste on a fixed mechanical toothbrush.

She had become adept at manipulating the strong twelve inches of upper arm she had on each side of her body. She pinched them together to carry larger items like pots. She folded books under her arm to carry them to her room, where she sat in bed for hours, knees pulled up to her chest, reading and turning pages with the eraser at the end of the pencil clenched in her teeth. These lay within easy reach in every room of the house for her. These were the tools she used for typing, or using remotes.

There were many things Ann still needed help with, of course. Sarah had brushed and pulled Ann's long brown hair into a tight braid, "This will have to do until I get back, honey." She had made a trip into town to stock up on books and food. She'd prepared more microwavable meals than Ann would be able to eat in a month. She'd made sure Dickerson's phone was left on its charger, her number programmed to call her with one button pushed. She'd even programmed the number of Scott's Pine Evangelical Church in case of dire emergency. She knew the pastor was a good man and would help Ann if needed.

Ann probably would have been just fine for the second week if something hadn't happened after the first one. She got bored. She'd read every book, both library or otherwise, in the house. TV held no interest for her. She still had plenty of food, but it all began to taste the same: bland, boring, frozen, thawed, boring. She wandered around the house aimlessly, watched the fish in her fish tank, then sat out under the elm tree talking to her father, wishing for his company. She recalled their conversation the morning he'd died and how he'd promised her things he'd not been able to give her, things she would love to have now: a cat to cuddle up to her when she was lonely, answers to the many questions that raced through her mind. Sarah had these answers, too. She longed for Sarah to come home.

Sarah called daily to check up on Ann and to tell her that things were going well. She wasn't yet sure when she'd be coming home, but it should just be another few days. Ann listened politely, convinced her not to hurry, that she was fine, and hung up feeling lonelier than ever. At the beginning of week two an idea she'd had before but never seriously considered popped into her mind. She was older now, capable, wiser, and she entertained it. By the middle of week two, her idea had formed into a plan. And by the beginning of week three, receiving Sarah's phone call giving the standard answer that it would still be a few more days resolved the issue. Ann was going to go into town.

Lola had raced the eight hours to the capital, anxious and excited. Frank was alive!   Memories of ten years of marriage flooded her mind. Trips they'd taken, joy rides in his car, their laughter together—these experiences had made them close and she was excited to pick up where they'd left off. The details she'd received from Reverend Phillips caused her some concern, but she was sure everything would be alright. She prayed they would be. Her confidence vanished when she saw him.

The reverend greeted her with a hug and walked her downstairs to the safe room. She saw him then and shook her head. This wasn't Frank. This was a confused old man with wild eyes and shaky hands. He stood up and walked toward her, recognition and relief lighting his face. He reached to pull her into an embrace. She hesitated until he whispered, "Lola, my love." His gentle voice melted her and she fell into his arms. She remembered him then, the fullness of him, the things she'd forgotten in their long, painful absence. She remembered how she fit perfectly into the space his arms left when they folded around her. She remembered how the palm of his large hand on the small of her back made her shiver. She remembered his chin resting on the top of her head as he towered over her. It was bearded now, but she remembered. They both cried and clung to one another.

The three of them sat down and began to fill each other in on the past nineteen years. Reverend Phillips spoke of the church's awakening and how they were still going strong, reaching out, seeing lives changed. He was most excited to tell Lola about their Psalm 68 Project to young mothers, how they were valuing life, including the mother's, by giving a genuine alternative to abortion—supporting women throughout their pregnancy and birth experience, helping to place the children in open adoption situations with followers of Jesus who continued to reach out, help and encourage them. "I knew you'd appreciate the fact that all we do is fully, openly disclosed and done in the light. These women aren't just commodities, they are precious daughters of God who are struggling in this life because of choices they've made or choices they were denied. We are pro-life in regards to the mother as well as the unborn child. Our care for them extends beyond the birth and even beyond the adoption."

"Oh, that's wonderful! I'm so glad to hear that women have other options!"

"Yes, about that. After you left with the baby, the well-dressed representative from their office, the one we'd planned to turn the baby over to, gave me a phone call. She asked why we'd run out, I told her we'd had a change of heart. She asked where the baby was now. I told her she was out of state and safe. She told me, and I quote, 'Well, as I'm sure you are aware, we are an internationally based ministry with contacts all over this nation. While it is of course your choice on what to do with the baby, we have some concerns about the way things were conducted and feel it is in the best interest of all involved if, should we see the child again, she should be immediately taken into our custody. We have discussed this with our representative city officials and they are implicitly supportive of our efforts. Now I hope you will be forthcoming with any information you have regarding their whereabouts.' I told them I was bound by clergy-client privilege and could not give any information. She said she understood and looked forward to working with our church in the future should we ever have a need again."

Lola shook her head, amazed at the boldness and audacity of the OFA. "They are incredibly smooth. Strong-arming you would have undermined the secrecy and false integrity of their 'ministry.' This approach left them smelling like roses yet let you know that they were not done looking for her, that she'd never be safe here again. I'm so glad I didn't bring her with me."

"Yes, OFA still seems like an impenetrable force. We have learned a bit over the years about who they are and what they have their hands into. We are still waiting on God to show us what to do with this information. It's not as simple as going to the proper authorities. Their pockets are lined and their greedy eyes look the other way."

Their attention was drawn to Frank then. He had slumped low into his chair, his eyes vacant, mouth slack, reliving the horror of the room and the black box so many years ago. The reverend apologized, "I'm so sorry, every time we mention even the name of the company it sends Frank back into the horror he experienced at their hands. It's very difficult to bring him back."

Frank slumped off the side of his chair onto the floor, pulled his knees to his chest and began crying uncontrollably. "Lola! I'm so sorry. I killed her. Oh, God! Lola. How could I?" Lola went to his side and tried to comfort him.

"Frank, it's me, Lola. I'm okay. See, you didn't kill me. I'm alive, darling. I'm right here."

"Yes I did! I remember it all! I did it!" He suddenly pushed her over and straddled her, his eyes manic. "I put my hands on your neck and I squeezed until you were dead!" The reverend saw too late that this was a flashback gone terribly real. He tried to pull Frank off of Lola, but Frank was incredibly strong and this crazed state made him even more so. He ran upstairs to get help.

Lola squeezed out the words through his tightening thumbs, "Frank, what do you smell?"

"What are you talking about? Shut up! You aren't being loyal!" But his hands relaxed a bit.

"Smell, Frank. In your memory, when you walk in the house and it's trashed. What do you smell?"

"I don't smell anything, Lola. Nothing."

"Frank, when I walked into the house there was a strange smell. A cologne of some sort I think. It wasn't yours; it was sweeter, muskier, minty. It was powerful and lingered, I know it did, even until you came home and saw

I was gone."

He took his hands off her and rolled off of her, remembering now. "Yes, in the memory where you were gone, I smell the Suit's cologne in the house."

She sat slowly up, squared herself and looked him deep in his eyes. "Frank, that is the real memory. Your false memory has no scent because it's not real. You didn't kill me, Frank. I'm right here. I'm right here."

Flooded with relief, he pulled her into an embrace, "I'm so sorry, Lola. So sorry."

When the reverend burst into the room with two young men from the church, they saw the two of them locked into an embrace, kissing. He motioned for them to leave quietly. This reunion was long overdue.

Hours later, sitting together on the couch in the safe room, she told him the whole story. How they'd left in the darkness of night and driven with the baby to the house in Scott's Pine. Reverend Phillips had a connection there who they never met but had left the key to the house and a note telling them how to get to the real estate agency the next day. Lola did so, money in hand. She filled out paperwork under her new name—Lola Longly became Sarah Stone. The story she concocted about having lost her identification in the move and having replacements on order coupled with her pleasant, open face were enough to get accounts set up.

Over the next months of setting up a household they learned the power of paying cash. The overlooked documentation was forgotten. Dickerson became Michael Turner should anyone ask, which no one did. He was content to hole up on the property and devoted his waking moments to the tiny love of his life, who he'd named after the mother he'd likely never see again. Neither of them could decide on a last name, nor did they see the necessity of one, so she remained Annabelle Laura.

He was her father before she could speak her first babbling, "Da, da, da." He did everything for her — changed her, fed her and danced with her around the living room. He spoke loving words to her and played games. Peek-a-boo morphed into hide and seek. They made forts and read books. They acted out plays for Sarah's delighted applause. He tucked her in each night with a prayer and she bounced in to wake him each morning for a bear hug.

Sarah cooked, cleaned, made their clothing, and spent hours caring for and talking with Ann about a million subjects. They were close, and while it was true that many of the things Sarah did for Ann were things a mother does for her child, it was more comfortable for Sarah to keep a bit of a clinical distance than to feel the ache of not having this "family" with Frank.

All this she told Frank now through tears. He pulled her close into his chest. "We're together now, my love. Oh Lola, you've done such a good thing saving Ann. You and Dickerson both. I'm so sorry I haven't been here for you, dear. But I am now. And I promise, if it's the last thing I do, I'll finish what I started those many years ago. I'll see to it that if that company is still in business, those people are still alive, I'll make them pay for what they've done! They'll pay, Lola!"

Lola pulled back at the wildness that entered his eyes

then. She rubbed her neck and shook her head. "Frank, you can't just go after them and get revenge. Not by yourself. Not without me." She pulled her purse off the floor and pulled it open toward Frank. He smiled when he saw what she'd hidden inside. His old .45.

It took Ann all morning to talk herself into walking out the front door. She stood there on the front step for another twenty minutes mustering the courage to go further. The end of the driveway was the point of no return for her. She'd never been further. She knew the gravel and paved roads meandered around properties for five miles before reaching town. She'd overheard Sarah comment that it was a shame a straight shot hadn't been cut out instead through the uninhabited woods on the other side of their road. It would have cut it down to a one mile journey. Ann took a deep breath and stepped across the imaginary line dividing her familiar world from all she was ignorant of and headed purposefully into the trees.

At the other edge of them she stopped and took it all in. On the other side of the tall scraggly jack pine she hid behind was a quiet, clean little town. Freshly painted buildings showcased colorful displays behind clean windows. The sidewalks and streets looked freshly swept, devoid of litter or even a stray fallen leaf or grass clipping. Hypnotized, she stared at a slowly revolving barber pole like the ones in the books she'd paged through with Sarah. Except they hadn't turned in the books. She blinked and shook her head angrily now. How much more was she ignorant of? Why had they kept her from this town, these people, any people? Feeling childish and small, she turned and ran for home. The familiarity of the four walls in her room first made her feel safe, but soon closed in again. She'd go back. She'd learn more. And when Sarah returned she'd get all the answers she deserved.

⌐⁊ℓ⌐

"We'll be coming home tomorrow, Ann." Sarah's voice on the phone was both comforting and alarming.

"We?"

"Yes, Frank is coming with me. My husband. It's such a long story and one I don't want to tell you on the phone. As soon as we get there we'll all sit down and talk. About everything."

"Everything?"

"Yes, everything. We should have told you long ago."

Ann hung up and thought about all that she'd have to tell Sarah, too. She hoped Sarah would understand, but was also prepared to stand her ground. Here she was, nineteen years old and she'd bravely gone out into the world on her own, made a friend and even gotten a job. A job!

The past few days had been a whirlwind of new experiences, her head still reeled from trying to sort it all out. She went to bed hoping it'd unscramble itself.

The next morning Ann again went to Mr. Howsen's store, just as she had since he'd walked up to her hiding in the tree line and tried to strike up a conversation with her.

She'd remained fearfully silent. "I won't hurt you, young lady. What's your name?" She stood, staring. "Where'd you come from?" He peered at her over the rim of his glasses, recognizing the material of her homemade jacket. She turned and wordlessly fled home.

The second day she'd stood in the shadows until he came out of his shop and waved her over. She stepped out shyly and walked to him. "Well, you sure don't say much, do you? You belong to Miss Sarah and that old hermit, don't you? I knew I'd seen that pretty pink denim before. I was starting to worry about Sarah. She hasn't been to town in a couple of weeks. She okay?" Ann nodded vigorously. "Well, I admit I'm surprised at her keeping such a big secret, but I guess she's got her reasons. It's not really any of my business, you know. Come in and I'll buy you a Coke."

She couldn't resist his kindness. She went in and sat on a stool at the tall counter he walked behind. He handed her a can, a straw and a glass of ice. She frowned, frustrated. "What is it, Miss?" Mr. Howsen peered over his bifocals again and smacked his forehead as understanding set in. "Oh, no! I'm so sorry. Lemme help you there." He poked the straw into her glass and poured the Coke into it. "That's better. How rude of me not to notice right away. I'm sorry."

She smiled at him gratefully and sipped. He wiped the counter with a white rag and kept the one-sided conversation going. "Yep, I never was very observant, even before I got old and had to get these glasses. My wife, God rest her soul, used to help me out all the time. She'd poke me in the ribs or clear her throat and I'd take a closer look.

That's how I managed to stop myself from congratulating women who weren't pregnant." Ann grinned, which encouraged him to go on, "That's how I introduced myself to my neighbor instead of his donkey, too." They both laughed then. "Oh, so you do make sound. Well, you've every right to be quiet if you want to. To each his own, I always say. Or to each her own, in this case. You're too pretty to mistake for anything else."

On the third day she walked right up to the store counter and nodded her head toward a piece of paper taped to the wall behind him. It was the flier he'd put up a few days ago. HELP WANTED: SIDEWALK SWEEPING. Surprised, he asked, "Are you telling me you want this job?" She moved her head up and down quickly, smiling. "Well, it doesn't pay much and it's pretty hard work. The boy who did it before went off to college in the city. I'm just not sure it'd be a good fit for you..." She frowned a little, pulled off her shawl, and he saw them for the first time. Her shirt sleeves ended like socks stretched around her deformed limbs. She confidently strode to the corner where he'd absently placed a broom. She wriggled it out from the wall and folded her muscular upper arms around, one behind, one in front—gripping it tight. She swished side to side, then, using her hips to force the broom right and left across the wooden floor.

Howsen stood, shocked, speechlessly watching her go from one side of the room to the other. She dropped the broom with a clatter against the wall and went next for the push broom. Fixing her arms as weights around it she walked forward with it from the back of the store to the front door, where she deposited the dirt out onto the street.

When she'd finished she looked stubbornly to Howsen for his decision. He faced away from her at the counter, quietly polishing his eyeglasses on his white apron. He cleared his throat, "I'm sorry I ever doubted you, Missy. The job's yours if you want it." She smiled and practically skipped out the door. Mr. Howsen blew his nose, wiped the last tear from the end of his chin and shook his head wonderingly at this new girl who'd come to town.

To say nothing exciting ever happened in Scott's Pine wouldn't be accurate. To say that absolutely nothing even remotely interesting ever happened would be closer to the truth. So much so that when a young man came into town one Monday morning and pulled his little blue Honda Civic into a parking spot in front of the cafe, he created an absolute uproar. Everyone in town was soon talking about the business that brought him, with his camera and tripod and little spiral bound notebook opened, taking notes as he asked questions and observed.

"He's here doing a story on Scott's Pine."

"Our town's been picked in the top one-hundred places in America to live."

"I hope this doesn't bring a bunch of strangers here."

This was an unwelcome turn of events for people like Sarah and Frank, who protected their privacy and that of Ann's. Since returning to the hermit house on the hill, the three of them had become a family of sorts. Ann immediately took a liking to the tall, gentle man who walked in the door with a large smile on his face and a little cat nestled in his arms. "This is Millie. Lola, er, Sarah said you wouldn't mind if I brought her, too."

Ann nuzzled her soft fur with her nose, "Hi, Millie." She straightened and turned to Sarah, "Hi Lola. Welcome home. I guess it's time for that talk."

"Yes, it is, Annabelle. Let me put some coffee on." Sarah smiled.

The four of them sat around the table, Millie curled on Ann's lap, and talked far into the night. Ann learned everything they knew. She'd been born in a makeshift delivery room in a warehouse secretly operated by OFA. They didn't know what they'd done with her mother. Frank thought the furnace he'd narrowly avoided was probably utilized for getting rid of the young women who birthed there, but he couldn't bring himself to tell her this.

Rejected for sale due to her birth defect, she was rescued, and given a new start in Scott's Pine. Finally she understood the secrecy and overprotectiveness of her father and Sarah. She loved them, and this new man, Lola's husband Frank, for what they'd done for her. "Thank you."

She told them about her adventures in town and was relieved to see pride in Sarah's eyes. "Of course you went into town. I'm so glad you met Mr. Howsen. He's a good man. But you can see now why we must remain careful not to talk to people about our past."

"Do you really think the company would come after us after almost twenty years?"

Frank spoke up, "I don't know. I know they wouldn't

want anyone to incriminate them. And until we know whether The Suit and Carpet Bagger are still in business, we don't want to alert them to the fact that we still exist."

"What do you mean? Are you planning to go after them?"

Frank glanced at Sarah. "You were right, she is very smart." He looked at Ann, "Yes. We have to stop them, Ann. You escaped because of a special set of circumstances..."

"You mean because of these," she flapped her arms up and down in disgust.

"Yes. Many babies were not so lucky. They were sold to the highest bidder for unspeakable things. And the mothers they preyed on were young, vulnerable, invisible. Dehumanized commodities in a brutal, disgusting business. They deserve justice."

It was the first time Ann had ever considered her disability as anything but a curse. "You're right. I'm coming, too. I won't take no for an answer."

Frank grinned at Sarah, "She really is your daughter!"

"We are a long way from going anywhere or doing anything, young lady. We must tread carefully."

"More careful than I was twenty years ago, walking in guns blazing."

"Yes, we'll know what to do when the time and situation is right. For now, let's lay low and see what we can find out about OFA and what they've been up to."

And so began the first phase of their plan, to research and compile as much information as they could while living as normally and discretely as possible in a town which would soon be receiving national attention.

He sat in a middle booth near the window, laptop open, a steaming cup of coffee sending rivulets of steam dancing up in little curlicues and waves. Mesmerized, he realized they were more interesting than the fluff piece he was writing about a nothing town with nothing happening and no one interesting in it. This had been his dream job until he'd gotten it. He'd expected to be writing in-depth coverage about exciting locations, giving the reader literary snapshots of experiences and adventures most people wouldn't have access to otherwise, or inspiring their own risk-taking spirits. But low man on the totem pole meant working his way up to those assignments.

He could see how this town had gotten picked as one of the 100 most idyllic settings in the USA, at least on paper. He'd seen the statistics. Almost no crime, fairly high average earned income, schools that scored high year after year in standardized testing and college attendance—add these facts to the beauty of the scenery in this part of the country and even his first impressions of a clean, orderly, friendly town and he could see why it'd been picked.

The interview he'd done with the town librarian had revealed a quaint founding father story that he'd use in his article. It turned out the industrious Scott Parlin had talked Frances Howsen and Roger McNab into buying up all the property in Clayburne County they could afford in order to start Parlin Paper Company. The three men stood in the center of their newly purchased land, surveying the endless trees and opportunity that were now theirs for the taking.

Roger pointed out a large tree nearby and quipped, "I do believe this is the oldest one here, just like you, old man."

Frances joined in, "Better not cut that one down, then. You know, out of respect for the elderly?"

"Shut up, the both of you. I'll show you young fellers what this old man can do." Scott Parlin grinned, grabbed his ax and felled the first tree without their help. First the stump, then the clearing, then the town that grew up around it were called Scott's Pine.

After being here only a few days the reporter was already beginning to see beneath the thin veneer. There was nothing dark and lurking—he almost wished there were for the sake of his boredom. It was more of an inbred loyalty people had to each other which both held a friendly hand out to shake an outsider's hand and another hand up to keep them at a distance. It was palpable, but he wasn't sure how or if to write about it. That sort of insight wasn't what the newspaper was looking for anyway. So he'd stick to the facts, write what they wanted, snap some pretty pictures, include some town history and move on. Hopefully to something with more teeth.

He sat up with a start when he saw her. Intrigued, he stared at her out the window as she came out of the store, broom clutched tight to her body, and began to sweep. She was wearing blue jeans and a sweatshirt that had clearly been hemmed to protect and hide the ends of her deformed arms. Her long brown hair was braided loosely and hung halfway down her slender hips, which swayed from side to side as she pushed the dirt away from the sidewalk in front of the store down the sidewalk out of sight.

He moved his eyes back to the mostly empty computer screen, sipped his cold coffee and tried to think of something, anything to write about this town. He gave up when she swished into view right in front of his window minutes later. He realized she'd crossed the street and was moving gracefully, working quickly down his side now. She whisked past the window without looking up or him looking away.

"Warm up?" the waitress held a coffee pot over his cup.

"Sure, thanks. Who is that?"

"Who? Oh, the girl? That's just Nubby."

"Nubby?"

"Yes, she doesn't talk or anything. Just sweeps the sidewalks every day. Old Mr. Howsen felt bad for her and gave her a job."

"Mr. Howsen, the store owner? Where did she come from?"

"Rumor is she belongs to the hermit."

"Hermit?"

"Yep, lives up on McNab Hill. Nobody's ever seen him. Moved here about twenty years ago. But his housekeeper comes to town almost every week. Sarah's real nice. They keep to themselves mostly. Probably how they've gotten along so well in this town. Most of us stick pretty much to ourselves."

"I've noticed. Um, thanks for the coffee." He stood up, closing his laptop, and threw a five dollar bill on the table.

He strode outside thinking that maybe there might be more to this town than he'd given credit for. Maybe there was a story here after all, if he could uncover it.

⁓✐⁓

Nobody came up McNab Hill. The townspeople respected the hermit's proclivity for private living. Sarah picked up their mail at the post office and they'd maintained the property themselves since day one. If a pipe broke, Sarah fixed it. And now that Frank was there, he stepped into upkeep and repair of the grounds and buildings. This meant that the new roof needed on the old house would be his project.

Dickerson had been too old to do it when it was first needed five years ago. Sarah overcame her fear of heights enough to go up and tack tarps down on the worst offending leaky spots and then scrambled down in a state of panicked hyperventilation. They'd discussed hiring a handyman then but neither of them were willing to bring a stranger into their refuge. What if he'd seen evidence of Ann, something they'd overlooked, or begun asking questions? What if he said something to someone else, which created questions of their own? So, the roof remained tarped, leaking into the attic from time to time into buckets Sarah dumped out continually during rainstorms and spring thaws.

This is where Frank was on Sunday morning when Sarah and Ann were gone at church, up on the peak of the roof, pulling up old shingles, surveying the water-damaged wood underneath, and preparing himself mentally for an incredibly big job. From this vantage point, he saw the blue Honda pull slowly up the winding driveway. He ducked his head down, flattened himself against the roof and listened as the visitor shut off the engine, opened and closed their car door, and walked briskly to the front door. The doorbell unanswered, the stranger knocked loudly, then shouted, "Sir, if you're home, I'm sorry to disturb you. I am a reporter from the City Sentinel doing a story on Scott's Pine and just wanted to ask you a few questions about your daughter, um, the girl who sweeps the sidewalks?"

He knocked some more, rang the doorbell a couple more times. Receiving no answer he yelled through the door, "I'm sorry to have bothered you, sir. I'll be leaving now."

Frank heard his car door open and peered carefully over the edge of the roof. He saw the young man sitting in his car, peering intently across the backyard, squinting to try to see something. Frank froze, helpless to stop him as he got out and walked quickly across the grass. He snapped a couple of pictures and returned to his car. Frank knew he'd be back and with a lot of questions. He wasn't sure what else to do besides wait for the car to leave and pray that those pictures wouldn't end up in the wrong hands, and that they hadn't already.

"I've got the Scott's Pine piece wrapped up and am sending it to you right now." He punched a couple of buttons on his keyboard and so finished his official assignment in this little town. "I've put in two weeks of time off with human resources. No, I'm just enjoying this part of the country more than I expected to and want to take some vacation time. I know what I said before but it turns out there may be more to this town than I expected. A girl? What do you mean, did I meet a girl? Not yet, but I'm about to." Tony Burton flipped his phone shut, clicked the corner "X" of the picture he'd uploaded to his laptop, closed it and stood to walk across the street to introduce himself to Nubby. The image of the crude wooden grave marker was etched in his mind like the words carved on its face. *Here lies a good, good man. He will be missed.* Whose body lay beneath the newly covered grave? And who was this girl?

## CHAPTER SEVEN

# The Romance

Besides being an extremely private person to begin with, now Ann had the added pressure of keeping the secrets she'd only recently become privy to. She went to work each day, spoke little to Mr. Howsen and nothing to everyone else. She knew the townspeople called her Nubby. She didn't really mind; her disability had defined her in every other way, why not in name as well? No one asked her to reveal her identity or even tried to strike up a conversation with her. She was the mysterious hermit's daughter who'd strolled into town, gotten the sympathy of the storekeeper, and didn't bother anyone. She also came silently to church and the library with Sarah, the kindly housekeeper who they trusted not because of their many interactions with her, but despite them. Folks who kept to themselves and their own were understood and respected in this town. People like reporter Tony Burton were not.

"I can't imagine why it's taking that young fellah so

long to finish up his story."

"He's been here for over a week and I saw him drive down from McNab Hill yesterday."

"Somebody ought to say something to him."

But no one did. They convinced themselves it was really none of their business, got busy with their own lives and avoided him. The cold shoulder that had turned so many visitors and prospective neighbors away over the years only served to increase Tony's drive to investigate further, stubbornly refusing to take the collective hint and back off. He couldn't, wouldn't, until he found some answers. Even though he was fairly certain there was no earth-shattering mystery to be solved, his curiosity and tenacity were sufficient to keep him in Scott's Pine a bit longer.

And then there was Nubby. It felt a little creepy, this obsession he'd developed. He watched her work, gliding back and forth along the sidewalks of town, jaw set in concentration for the task at hand. He imagined it couldn't be easy for her to keep up the pace the job demanded of her. Yet he saw she was a hard worker, not a charity case. Mr. Howsen got what he paid for, clean sidewalks from one end of town to the other each week. He watched from his window vantage point in the cafe as she worked. Once he saw her grip slip on the handle of the broom and it clattered noisily to the ground. He stood quickly in response to the surprising desire to rush out and pick it up for her, then squelched it and sat down as he saw her move her shoe deftly underneath the wood and slide it up until it was at a high enough angle for her to wriggle it back into place. She continued working as if nothing had happened. He looked on, his admiration for her growing with each passing day, along with his desire to meet her.

He couldn't explain his lack of nerve. Usually he was very outgoing and confident—excellent qualities for a reporter to have. But meeting her gave him an anxiety that was totally new to him. He brushed it off as being sensitive to her disability, not wanting to inadvertently say something stupid or patronizing to her. He picked the imaginary words he would say to her and looked on, more and more afraid of screwing things up with her, and more and more confused about why he even cared.

She'd seen him watching her. Sarah had flashed Frank a look when Ann told them about it at the dinner table. "Just be careful. The last thing we really need is a nosy reporter finding out who we really are. He hasn't been back up here yet but he will be. Just ignore him and he'll go away," Frank reassured her. Neither Sarah nor Ann were convinced, however; Sarah, because she knew it was more than curiosity that drew him. It was also the fact that Ann was a beautiful girl worthy of the pursuit of a man's heart. Ann, because she'd seen the intensity of his gaze, even from across the street, behind the reflection of the glass.

So it didn't surprise her when he sauntered out the door of the diner the next morning and strode up to her. She pretended not to notice him and continued sweeping. Without thinking, he stuck out his hand to shake hers, "Hi, I'm Tony...Idiot." Realizing what he'd done, he plunged his hand into his pocket, turned around and walked shamefully back to the diner, muttering under his breath.

What she didn't see was how he could have cried from embarrassment and disgust with himself. What he didn't see was her smile as she lowered her head and continued her work.

The next day he watched sorrowfully from his window vantage. Fall was coming on, its chilly fingers wrapped around her as she worked, her breath exhaled in crystalline puffs. She had a purple stocking cap pulled over her ears, and try as he might, he couldn't resist thinking about how cute it was on her, how her cheeks looked soft and rosy, pinched by the same frost that had harassed him when he'd stepped out of the motel room early this morning. He watched her lips, pursed in concentration, then relaxed, full, pink, inviting—he slammed his coffee cup down suddenly, giving the other patrons a start. He stood, embarrassed and disgusted with himself, a grown man sitting there mooning over a beautiful girl. He was a man of action, he told himself. It was time to take it.

Tony bought a coffee to go, grabbed a straw and headed across the street to Nubby. Confident and sure, he boldly walked up to her and stammered, "Um, hi. I'm Tony, we met yesterday, well, I tried to, well, I was just..." She had stopped sweeping and stood politely, looking at him. He laughed nervously, his voice sounding high pitched and weak to his mortified ears. "Here, I got this for you." He hurriedly placed the warm drink on the top of a nearby tall blue postal box. "I hope you like coffee. I like coffee." He retreated then, his words echoing in a million whiny, nerdy, decidedly unmasculine, unattractive voices ...I like coffee...I like coffee...I like coffee. "Tony Idiot, indeed!" he muttered as he nearly broke into a run, escaping his shame.

Ann watched him, amused and a bit intrigued, too. Who was this stranger in town and what did he want with her? Sarah and Frank had warned her not to talk to him, that he could jeopardize their covers. She knew he'd been to their house and snapped pictures of her father's gravesite. But his behavior toward her wasn't one of a man matter-of-factly pursuing a story. So what was he after then? And why was she looking forward to their next bumbling meeting?

She sipped carefully through the straw, grateful for the hot drink as it warmed up her belly. It was the first gift she'd ever received from someone other than her father or Sarah. In an existence where she was mostly ignored, it was welcome. She felt her heart warming, opening a little at the thought of a man who may actually be interested in her. This entirely unexpected, novel thought fueled her as she worked throughout the day. By the time she was finished, all she could think about was getting home to tell Sarah about him.

When she got home, she was shocked to see his car in their driveway. Millie wrapped herself around Ann's legs, purring and begging for attention as Ann walked from room to room searching for them throughout the house. But neither the visitor, Sarah, nor Frank were anywhere in sight.

⁕

They had a carefully constructed plan for his imminent return. The most important thing to them was still Ann's safety and security, seconded by their own. Their plans to take out the OFA couldn't be executed if their identities were blown, so they vowed to do whatever it took to keep the man quiet. First they needed to find out what he already knew. So, they waited, and when his silver car meandered up McNab Hill, they were prepared. Frank hid in the bedroom within earshot, the loaded .45 holstered by his side.

Sarah met him at his car. "Hi, I'm Sarah Stone. Can I help you?"

"Hi, I'm Tony Burton, from the City Sentinel. I'm here in Scott's Pine doing a story and wondered if I could have a few minutes of your time?" They shook hands.

"Sure, come on in, I have some fresh coffee on. My name's Sarah. I live here in the carriage house."

"That'd be great! Thank you!" He followed her up the steps into her little apartment. "This is a nice place you've got here."

"Yes, we've been here about twenty years, as I'm sure the townspeople have told you." She motioned toward a chair at the table. He sat, his back to the bedroom.

"Yes, they told me a few things, but not much. Folks are pretty private around here. Ma'am, would you mind if I get right to the point?"

"Call me Sarah and yes, I'd actually prefer it." She smiled, placed a mug in front of each of them and sat down. "I can't imagine why you've returned to McNab Hill. We're outsiders here, hardly the folks who could give you anything helpful for your piece on Scott's Pine."

It was his turn to smile. He fidgeted, picked his words carefully, and then blurted, "Who is she?"

"What do you mean?" Sarah was surprised by his bluntness.

"The beautiful girl in town, the sweeper. They call her Nubby and the waitress at the cafe told me she belongs to you and the hermit up here, but who is she? **I have to know who she is!**" This last statement came out louder than he'd intended. In the bedroom, Frank silently pulled his gun from its holster.

"Have you spoken to her?"

"No, I tried, but I got all tongue tied." He shook his head miserably.

Sarah smiled. "Well, if she wants to be known by you, I think she should be the one to decide how much so." She leaned closer to him, searching his eyes for the truth, "You're not still here to work on a story about the town, are you, Mr. Burton?"

"No, ma'am. I'm not. I was hoping to learn more about the girl."

"Why?" Frank hid against the inside of the doorway, pressed hard against the wall, gun held at the ready, listening intently for the young man's answer.

"I, um. I never met anyone like her before. I don't know, she intrigues me." He looked up at her, face crimson with the embarrassment of his confession. "Sounds dumb, I know."

"No, not dumb. But you are going about this wrong, I must say. I would think that you of all people should know that if you want to know more about someone, you need to go to the source. I will tell you one thing, though. She is like a daughter to me, and if you are trying to get close to her for any purpose other than to befriend her, we will protect her. Do you understand, young man?"

Tony could tell this was more than the good natured ribbing of a protective parent. He caught full well the threat in her undertone and nodded. "I would never try to hurt her, Sarah. Never." His voice rang with sincerity.

Frank relaxed and holstered his gun. Sarah reached across the table and patted his hand. "I know, dear."

She walked him out to his car then. "Thank you for the coffee, Sarah. And for the advice."

"You're welcome, Tony." She patted him on the back before he climbed into his car and drove back down the hill.

Ann watched from her upstairs window. When his car was out of sight she bounded downstairs and over to Sarah's apartment. "What did he want?" Sarah looked at Frank for help, but he grinned, shrugged his shoulders and walked out the front door, stifling a chuckle.

"He is investigating a particularly interesting lead," Sarah replied.

"What do you mean? Did he ask about the grave?"

"No, he didn't."

"Did he ask about Father and you and how you came to Scott's Pine?"

"No, he didn't ask about those either."

Indignant now, Ann demanded, "Well then, what could be so interesting that he'd drive all the way up here? What did he ask about?"

Sarah walked to her, grabbed her shoulders gently and looked into her eyes. "He asked about you, dear."

The storm blew in late that night, winter making a premature statement of its intentions. Ann was awakened by the force of it slamming into the side of the house. Outside her window trees waved wildly, scratching and clawing at each other, at the building, at empty air. But they barely got her attention. She snuggled deeper under her blankets and dreamily replayed Sarah's words. "He asked about you, dear," and fell back to sleep.

The next morning it took Ann twice the time it usually did to walk into town. She had to skirt around downed trees, branches scratching at her legs. Her usual trail was unrecognizable in the aftereffects of the winds that had toppled trees, ripped apart power lines and made most roads in and out of Scott's Pine impassable.

She heard the chainsaws working before she got there. Townspeople had come early to clear away trees. There had been no serious damage done, but the streets and sidewalks were a mess. Ann looked on and mentally calculated the hours it would take to clear; she couldn't. Instead she shook her head, picked up her broom at Mr. Howsen's store, walked to the end of the block and started working.

Her usual method of cleaning was to start on one side of town, make a straight line from the south to the north end, cross the street and do the other side. This cleared the main street first. Then she crisscrossed back and forth, east to west. In a typical week, she could get the entire town finished by herself. She realized quickly that this would not be a typical week when it took her the first four hours just to get halfway up Main Street.

She went into the diner to take a lunch break. She ordered her food and sat back in the break room. She didn't like to eat in front of anyone because of her unconventional methods and the stares and comments she'd gotten the first and only time she'd eaten in public. The waitress had offered her the break room then, saying "We don't use it during the lunch rush, so you'd have it all to yourself, honey."

⟋⁘⟍

Tony watched her go into the diner, then walked purposefully over to the store. "Yes, I'd like one of these, please," he hurriedly put the item on the counter and dug out some cash from his pocket.

"Okay, that'll be twenty-five dollars. Good luck, young man," Mr. Howsen said, smiling knowingly.

"Thanks." Tony was all the way outside before what the man had said registered. *Good luck? What was that all about?* He decided to ask the man later. Now he had other things to do.

Ann took a deep breath before stepping out the door of the diner to go back to work. This was going to be an incredibly long day, her entire body was already tired.

She walked to where she'd left off with her broom.

There it was, sitting against the wall right where she'd put it, but the sidewalk was already cleared. In the distance, on the far north side of town, she saw a tall figure pushing debris into the street. She marched toward him, trying to decide whether to be angry or grateful for this person who was taking over her job. When she got closer she paused—it was him.

Tony stopped sweeping and looked at Ann. She was stoic, her face unreadable. He hoped his bold move hadn't served to push her farther away. He said the first thing that popped into his mind, "I thought you could use a hand." His hand clamped over his mouth in horror. He'd done it again!

He stammered an apology, "Oh, I am such an idiot, I'm sorry, I just meant..." She walked past him to the littered walkway, hiding a smile, and began swinging her broom back and forth. He stood there, loathing himself for a moment, then joined her. They worked in silence for the rest of the day, side by side.

This continued the rest of the week. He met her in the morning and they set to work. The second day he ventured to speak up, "I'm really sorry I don't know how to talk to you without saying something stupid. Do you mind if I try again?" She glanced up quickly and he took that for permission. "My name is Tony Burton and I came here on an assignment for the City Sentinel. Our travel section featured Scott's Pine as one of the one-hundred best places to live in America."

She kept working. "It really is beautiful here. In fact I find some aspects to be absolutely breathtaking." He almost whispered this and she felt her cheeks blush a little. "So I stayed a couple extra weeks, took some vacation time." He rambled now, but she seemed to be listening and he was glad to have her attention. "The first week I explored and relaxed and then there was the storm. I am staying until the end of this week, going back to the city on Friday. The roads should be all cleared by then."

This news was disappointing. She wondered how much of a friendship was possible or practical to develop in only a week. She swept harder, biting her lower lip.

"I'll be able to help you with all of the cleanup I think. If you want me to, I mean."

Ann looked at him, screaming "yes!" with her eyes, hoping he could read them, but unwilling to break her silence. Not yet. She had to be sure. But he was looking down again, focused on their work.

But he showed up the next day, and the next, and then it was Friday. She woke up that morning with a sense of dread. They would be completing the last street today and he'd be leaving that night.

She'd heard all about him this week, where he was from, funny stories about his family, his plans for the future. She knew he wasn't satisfied, challenged in this, his first job out of journalism school. She knew he was intelligent, hard-working and humorous. She knew he had an inquisitive mind and that it was agonizing for him to know nothing about her.

When he came running up balancing two cups of coffee in one hand and their brooms in another, he stopped short at the look in her face.

"Ann," she said simply.

He stepped closer. "Ann?"

She nodded, smiling. "Yes, my name is Ann."

"Hi, Ann. I'm so very glad to finally meet you." He realized he was, with all his heart.

That day Ann talked. She told him about her favorite books, silly stories about pets she'd had, her future goals. He didn't ask her anything personal though his head was swimming with questions. He was afraid he'd spook her, and took every bit of information she shared about herself as a precious gift. He found her to be well-educated on every subject they discussed, witty, and kind hearted.

When they finished the last bit of the cleanup effort, he told her he wasn't ready to leave Scott's Pine just yet and asked if she was available for a walk on Saturday. He'd leave Sunday morning to get home and back to work Monday.

Without thinking, she invited him to McNab Hill to spend the day together, which he accepted. Only later, walking home did she consider the problems involved in keeping their lives secret. She steeled herself to tell Sarah and Frank about her rash invitation.

They had had this discussion already, they said. Their impressions were that Tony Burton was a trustworthy man whose attention was on her, not on blowing a story about their pasts. In the interest of her getting to live her life, have friends, maybe even romance (this part embarrassed Ann), they knew they needed to open up the tight hold they had on their homes and lives. If Ann felt he was safe enough to invite home for the day, they trusted her judgment and were willing to let her take the lead in what was okay to share with him.

Frank's only stipulation was that if he had to hide in the apartment all day, he should like to be at least visited by his sexy wife (this part embarrassed Sarah). "Oh, and I must have pizza." They all laughed.

When Tony arrived, Ann told him she wanted to show him something. She led him to the backyard and the simple grave that honored her father. She explained that she knew this wasn't a typical resting place for a loved one, maybe it wasn't even legal, but this had been his final wish, to be buried here under his favorite tree behind the house he'd loved to spend endless hours in. She told him about her father then. Their games, his love of jazz, how beautiful he'd made her feel with his words and kind eyes. Tony found it easy, here in her presence, to shut down his inquisitive nature and just listen—to her words, to her story, to her heart.

They walked for a while, her teaching the city boy what she knew about the trees, the history of Scott's Pine, the paper company and the people. Most of it he'd heard before, researched, read, listened to others' versions. But through her perspective it was all new. He soaked it in, lost in her accounts, lost in her lilting voice, lost in the hope of her next glance, her attention focused on him.

They'd eaten dinner together with Sarah, and he knew this was her at the most vulnerable she'd allowed herself to be with him, maybe with anyone. Sarah left silverware next to his plate, but he joined them in their unconventional eating methods. They slurped soup through straws. He ate his bread and pre-cut meat and potatoes by bending down and pulling them in with his lips, mimicking her graceful movements. His were less practiced and polished, and they laughed at Millie as she batted the little pieces he dropped on the floor. They watched a movie together, sitting close on the couch.

She walked him to his car and he awkwardly pulled her into a quick hug before leaving, "Can I call you tomorrow? And the next day? And probably the one after that?" She laughed and nodded.

But away from her the next day, alone on the trip back to the city, the spell lifted. Questions surfaced one after the other. Why wasn't her father's name on the wooden cross? Where had they come from, this mysterious hermit, housekeeper and baby, and why? When he'd first talked to Sarah, how had she known he'd been up to their house before? And what did she mean when she said "they" would protect her? Another thing, who'd fixed the roof that had been torn apart the first time he'd driven up McNab Hill?

He had to know the truth about Ann. His instincts told him there was much more to this story. He wouldn't stop until he found out what it was. All of it.

# PART THREE

# LIGHT

CHAPTER EIGHT

# The Investigation

He did call the next day. And the one after that. Every night, in fact, they talked, their discussions permeated with the comfortable silences of new friends who were actively listening, letting things sink in, mulling them over in their minds, and enjoying putting them in invisible categories labeled "endearing" and "even more endearing."

He told her about the newspaper, his co-workers and boss. He told her about his favorite restaurants and places he loved to visit in the city. He told her about how he missed Scott's Pine, its well-kept streets and pretty little white board houses. He told her he missed her.

She told him about the books she'd been reading. She told him about the beauty of the snow on the pines. She told him about the townspeople, how Mr. Howsen asked about him, teasing her. She told him she missed him.

Meanwhile, the three of them were doing as much online research as they could on OFA and not getting far.

They found a professional website for Overseas Franchise Administration. It highlighted a trade business specializing in the importing and exporting of natural resources worldwide. Just as they expected, it gave them no clues as to any behind the scenes operations or the man at its head.

They also found an archived site for One For All. It hadn't been updated in five years. It looked nothing like the first website, but was a lower budget do it yourself site. One tab, titled "Pregnant Women," linked to the smiling faces of young women giving testimonials about how they didn't know where to turn with their unwanted pregnancies until they'd found the kindness of One For All. Another tab was titled "Pro-life" and detailed the mission of the organization to reach out to the lost and forgotten young women tragically affected by rape and the after-effects of an unwanted pregnancy. "We exist to serve an underserved population of young women in our city who desire to birth their baby rather than abort it."

Another tab was called "Confidentiality." It outlined the specific services OFA would provide. "We are a privately funded resource available to homeless, drug addicted, runaway, invisible young women who have nowhere to turn, no family or community resources open to them. Many are referred to us by churches. We take them in and provide them with a home, prenatal care, birthing support, postnatal care and either parenting education or adoption options, all at no cost to them, the church, or taxpayers."

Reading between the lines disgusted Ann, Frank and Sarah. "These people prey on the marginalized, the lowest socioeconomic groups in our city, and come out looking like heroes," Frank looked earnestly at the two women.

Sarah added, "They use the general apathy of a busy, self-centered society to supply their baby mills. Even churches are quick to find an easy answer for the women who appear on their doorsteps asking for help." She remembered Reverend Phillips eagerly bounding in to tell them about the OFA option for baby Ann.

"And protecting their confidentiality becomes the smokescreen covering up their true intentions and actions. They take in women like my mother, let them give birth to babies who will be sold to the highest bidder, and dispose of her. Getting rid of any evidence of her life isn't difficult. She never had one to begin with. She looked up through tears at them. "If I hadn't been disabled, I would have been used. I would have been thrown away. Just like my mother. We have to stop them. People have to know about this."

"That's why we're going to the city, Ann. We are going to get the information we need and we are going to bring them down. I don't know how yet. As you can see it's almost impossible to find anything on these people. They cover their tracks so well. But we have to try." Frank leaned over and kissed her on the forehead. "I can't even think about what you were rescued from. I'm just glad you were."

"Thanks to you!"

"Thanks to God!" Sarah smiled. "And we will be used to rescue more. No matter what it takes." She became silent suddenly, staring into space.

"What is it, Sarah?" Ann asked, concerned.

"I just remembered something Reverend Phillips said when I went back for Frank: 'We have learned a bit over the years about who they are and what they have their hands into.' I think it's time we knew what he knows."

"I'm coming this time, Sarah. I want to help."

"I'm sure the opportunity to see a certain travel reporter has nothing to do with your motivation, right?" Frank teased.

"Well, maybe a little," Ann conceded.

"It's settled then. We have some calls to make. We're going back to finish this. Once and for all." They all grimaced at his accidental pun.

Reverend Phillips had set up the conference room for them. They sat down around a large rectangular table with him. Frank, Sarah, Ann were on one side, a printed out report, notebook and pen lying in front of each of them. Three spots remained on the opposite side—one for the reverend, and two empty chairs with identical supplies in front of them. "The other two men will be here shortly."

Ann was excited for this initial meeting to be over with. She'd made plans with Tony to meet for lunch. She stuck the pen in her teeth and doodled on the paper in front of her while they waited. She had learned to write this way, and had surprisingly beautiful penmanship. Frank and Sarah looked on, smiling at her thinly veiled nervousness, remembering the feelings of their own young romance thirty years ago. Frank gave her hand a little squeeze under the table.

"I brought a private investigator in. He's retired, but

the best in the business and a close personal friend of mine. In the past I have trusted him with my life."

An older man walked in then and finished his sentence for him: "...and yours."

Their mouths dropped open with surprise. Mr. Howsen grinned at their expressions as he embraced Reverend Phillips. "Hello, brother. I guess we have some explaining to do, eh?"

Sarah laughed, "I always wondered who your Scott's Pine connection was!"

"Wait a minute, how do you two know each other?" Frank looked thoroughly confused.

"I think I know." Ann addressed Mr. Howsen. "Your wife was Reverend Phillip's sister, wasn't she?"

"Yes, ma'am! Over the years we've helped quite a few folks who needed an escape plan out of the city, haven't we, Bobby?" He slapped Reverend Phillips on the back good-naturedly.

"Bobby?" the room echoed, then laughed.

"Yes we have, Terence," Reverend Phillips countered, then asked, "Now that we're all on first name basis, let's give our associate a couple more minutes, shall we? I think his input will be very valuable to our little inner circle here."

Mr. Howsen sat and answered a few incredulous questions. He explained that the real reason the hermit house had seen such a quick turnover of occupancies was because it had served as an undercover outpost for the domestic violence escapees Sparta Baptist had funneled through the small town over the years. It was the perfect temporary setting for an anonymous person to begin a new life. Folks rarely pried. As long as the outsiders moved on, they didn't bring on suspicion.

"You knew about Ann all those years," Sarah said.

"I knew about a man and woman escaping with a baby. I figured out she was a girl when Sarah bought all that pretty material. And I knew who she was right away when I saw her standing at the tree line," Howsen said.

"I just recently asked him to help find out more about OFA," said Reverend Phillips. "I have personally gone to almost every church in the city, compiling what information I could gather from the pastors and leaders who'd had dealings with the company. What I found will shed light on the facade they've developed over the years regarding their false ministry angle, but I hit nothing but dead-ends when it came to the OFA corporation itself. As Frank can tell you, nosing around in their business is dangerous business, and I knew it was time to call in someone more qualified than a simple pastor in these matters."

"And everybody knows I have a hard time minding my own business!" Mr. Howsen quipped, rewarded with their laughter.

There was a knock at the door. "Come in!" Reverend Phillips said, then he and his brother-in-law got up as if on cue. "If you'll excuse us for a moment, I think you four will want to be alone." They walked out as the young man entered.

*※*

Upon his return to the paper, Tony's editor called him

into the office one morning with a request, "You did a fine job on the Scott's Pine piece."

"Thank you, sir."

"I know you are hoping to write more than just travel articles. I have an assignment for you if you are interested."

"Yes, sir!" Tony was excited to hear what he'd be working on next. The possibilities were endless—politics, special interest groups, criminal investigations. He'd even love to cover a sports story or local humanitarian effort. He wasn't prepared for what his boss said next, and recovered quickly to hide his disappointment.

"I'd like you to do a spinoff article on the recent CNN poll stating that of the three out of five young people who do not proclaim personal faith, ninety-five percent of them used to be in Christian churches."

"You want me to do an article on religion?"

"I want you to find out why there has been a mass exodus of Christians from the Christian Church in our Christian culture in recent years. I want facts, Tony, not conjecture or distorted polls or the opinions of either antiquated thinkers or modern skeptics."

"I don't understand, sir. What kind of facts am I looking for? What am I really trying to find out, here?"

"Put it this way...if indeed Christians are professing to follow Christ, and they are leaving the building, why is it? Have our evolved public policies and rational thinking pushed Him out, as well?"

"So, sort of an 'Elvis has left the building' effect?"

"Exactly. Not that I ever believed in Elvis, er, God in the first place, but many did, and now they don't. So what's going on? Do you want it or not?"

"I'll take it, sir. It's just not really what I expected."

"Life rarely is."

⌒ℳ⌒

"So let me get this straight. You are doing a piece on the relevancy of the church in our modern culture? Why don't you come down to our community night and interview some folks, see what we're about here. Then you can be the judge."

He listened attentively to the man on the other end of the phone. "Yes, your research is correct. We have seen a substantial increase in our numbers over the past five years where other churches have been struggling to hold onto their regular attenders. I really can't explain it, or take credit for it, for that matter. Come down Wednesday and we'll talk more."

Tony took him up on the offer and showed up at Sparta Baptist Church the next week. He felt instantly at ease when volunteers greeted him, shook his hand and asked him if he was hungry. They all sat down to a family style meal together, him and about thirty others, a hodgepodge of social, economic, racial and religious diversity.

He interviewed them as he ate. A Mormon man came here each week for a meal. Last week he'd gotten prayer from an eight-year-old girl who had been pouring drinks for them. He didn't know whether she was a volunteer or guest. He just knew she had released healing power when she'd touched him with her little hand and asked Jesus to touch him with His big one. He folded and unfolded his elbow, showing Tony, "See, it don't hurt anymore."

A woman chimed in, "I heard about this church from my friend. She used to have arthritis real bad, but they prayed for her and now she's like a young woman again.

"They? Do you mean the pastor and elders or whatever they're called?"

"No, just the regular people. Mostly the children or other people who've been spiritually touched themselves in some way, either emotionally or physically. Now my friend prays for others and they get healed, too."

"I've heard about this stuff happening in the Bible, but not nowadays. Why isn't everybody freaking out if all this, um, supernatural stuff is going on around here?"

She laughed a little. "Well, if you think about it, in our view His natural is super, but in God's economy, the super is natural."

"Yeah, I guess so. So, the pastor must be some kind of charismatic, mover and shaker. I bet he really stands out in a crowd, huh?"

"You tell me, you've already met him. He dished up your pot roast."

⁓

"What's he doing here?" The two men looked out over the crowd visiting comfortably over their home-cooked meals.

"Who? The reporter? He's here to do a story on church growth or lack thereof. He's going to interview me later tonight."

"Can you wait and invite him to our meeting in the morning?"

"Um, yes, but what does he have to do with our investigation?"

"You'll see. My how the plot thickens," Mr. Howsen rubbed his hands together delightedly.

Tony was usually very prompt, but he ran late for the Sparta Baptist Church meeting because he'd changed his shirt no less than five times in anticipation for his reunion with Ann later that day. He couldn't decide which she'd like. Then he couldn't decide which he even liked. Exasperated and tardy, he rushed to the church.

The receptionist directed him to the conference room where he politely knocked on the door, mentally rehearsing his apology. "Come in!" he heard and opened it.

Two men brushed past him. "Hi, Tony. Go on in, she's waiting for you."

"Thanks. Mr. Howsen? She? What's going on?" he asked incredulously. Glancing into the room his eyes locked on hers. "Ann?"

In unison they asked, "What are you doing here?"

Frank and Sarah stood, excusing themselves. "We're gonna go find some coffee."

Alone, Tony sat down next to Ann. "I'm working on a story for the religion section. I'm supposed to be interviewing Reverend Phillips. What's going on, Ann?"

"I'm sorry, Tony. I haven't been totally upfront with you. I wasn't sure I could trust you and I held back, but I can see you've been drawn into this despite me."

"No, I'm the one who's sorry, Ann. I haven't told you everything either. I had some questions about your past and didn't know how to ask you. I have been doing some digging since I got back to the city."

"You have? What have you found out?"

"A few things. None of it makes much sense to me yet, but I have a feeling that's soon going to change."

"Let's go get the others back in here. It's time for answers. I promise I won't hide anything from you again, Tony. To start with, my full name is Annabelle Laura, not just Ann."

"It's beautiful," he said softly. "No last name, Annabelle Laura?"

"Nope. I'm uncomplicated that way."

"That may be the only way," he chuckled. "In the interest of full disclosure I'll tell you one of my deepest, darkest secrets."

"Okay," she steeled herself for his admission.

"Leonard."

"Leonard? I don't understand."

"That's my actual first name, after my father. Tony is my middle name." He looked at her sheepishly.

"I'll never tell," she reassured him. They grinned.

⌒か⌒

After first filling each other in on the intricate ways

they were all connected to one another and to Ann's story, they compiled a list of all the facts they had on OFA, both branches. It was indeed a discouragingly small amount of information for twenty years of searching, sadly lacking in proof.

Reverend Phillips had heard multiple testimonies of churches and families who'd been duped into encouraging young women into the One For All ministry, only to lose contact with them permanently. Trying to find them or information about them or their babies was like explaining to the police that an invisible person had vanished. Missing Person reports were misfiled or not even filled out by a system that protected confidentiality and privacy. "We have no reason to believe OFA is doing anything illegal, immoral or anything less than a great service to our community." This was the standard reply they'd gotten from the authorities, and devoid of evidence to the contrary, they were forced to accept this answer.

Tony spoke up then, "Sarah, or should I say, Lola, did you know there was a missing person's report done on you?" He had the room's full attention. "That's how I began to unravel a bit of Ann's story. I searched the national database from around the time you and Dickerson appeared in Scott's Pine, just in case. I had an inkling you may have come from this part of the country. Accents never lie, you know." He smiled, then added, "There was a second missing person unaccounted for."

"Me," Frank said confidently.

"Nope, sorry, Frank. A nurse. Police broke down her door and saw evidence her house had been ransacked, an empty bottle of sleeping pills lay next to her bed, but she was nowhere to be found."

Frank remembered the nurse with the tortured, kind eyes who'd helped him escape all those years ago and spoke up, "I bet those bastards got rid of her body and any evidence of her working for them!"

The men in the room noticed the two women crying and moved to comfort them. Sarah was overcome with the idea that her family had been looking for her, had probably given up the search long ago. Ann was overcome with the sacrifice of her father, and of Sarah, the only family she'd ever had. Until now, she thought, as she looked around the room.

～

"I know how to get to him," Frank told Sarah later as they lay in bed. "I know how to lure him to the quarry."

"What about the old woman? Where do you think she is?"

"I don't know, but I'm confident Howsen and Tony can figure it out."

"And by the time they do, we'll have taken care of The Suit. Together."

Frank squeezed her hand under the blanket, "Of course, together."

～

For all their footwork, pounding the streets, questioning people and even staking out the OFA building, their big break came through an accidental discovery by Ann, sitting alone in the library reading through archived newspaper articles from two decades ago up to the present.

The article read:

*SENILE HOARDER FOUND ALONE IN APARTMENT CLUTCHING CARPET BAG. Police were called to the scene of a downtown apartment building for a reported domestic disturbance late Thursday evening. They broke in the door of an approximately 60 year old woman and pushed through towering piles of mildewed romance novels stacked from floor to ceiling. They found her cowered in a corner, screaming and in need of immediate medical attention. The large carpet bag she carried held no identification. Authorities are still trying to find out who she is. Any information can be directed to the Sheriff's office. She has been transported to the Sandstone Sanitarium for further observation.*

Ann called Tony and Mr. Howsen, "I think I've found her."

"What will you do now, Ann?"

"Now I go have a little talk with the woman who killed my mother."

"I'm coming with you, Ann. We'll do it together." Tony assured her.

And they did.

CHAPTER NINE

# The Confrontations

Gray. It described the sum of both the surroundings and the somber moods they found themselves in as they surveyed them. Ancient stone possibly carved from the quarry meant to be her grave twenty years ago towered above the nondescript landscape. The architectural monstrosity sat, cold and emotionless, its flat affect contagious.

Ivy on its black mildewed face hung loosely, colorless, as if it had decided to give up its grip, a gray sky its dreary backdrop. The soil looked like concrete, barren and hard. Wintry, lifeless trees struggled to break free from its grip, reaching skinny trunks and crooked finger-branches up and away, waving wildly to be noticed, rescued from this landscape devoid of beauty. Stuck they remained, however, their ancient vines hanging dejectedly.

"Are you sure you want to do this?" Tony asked gently.

"Yes, I have to."

He didn't understand, but he supported her fully. She gave him a grateful smile as he opened the door for her to enter. The heat had been cranked high in this building, radiators knocked, the dust they'd burnt off clung in the air. Hot air from the difficult to control system met their faces. But they both felt an icy chill down their backs as they walked into the Sandstone Sanitarium.

He wouldn't be able to resist the cryptic message they'd had delivered to his office. "I KNOW WHAT'S AT THE BOTTOM OF THE LAKE. COME ALONE TOMORROW MORNING." Frank and Sarah were as sure he wouldn't be alone as they were that he'd come. She took lookout at the top of a nearby hill while he waited at the edge of the quarry. She called him with the vehicle's arrival on the distant country road. "Frank, be careful. I love you."

"I will. You, too, honey. Call me if you see anyone else. I just need ten minutes alone with him. That'll be more than enough." He double-checked his firearm, hid it back in his pocket, satisfied it was ready, and stood facing the overgrown road, watching the black Phantom as it drove slowly up to him, stopped, and The Suit stepped out cautiously.

"Hello, Frank."

"Let's make this short, shall we? You're going to give me answers and I'm going to let you go."

"Let me go? Is this a hostage situation, Frank? Because

I thought we were just going to talk like men. I have questions of my own, and then I'll let her go."

Frank's eyebrows shot up in alarm. "What are you talking about?"

"Your wife, Frank. Did you really think we wouldn't see her up there? Intercept your cell phone frequencies? Oh, don't worry, I'm sure you'll get your ten minutes alone with me. And my associate will enjoy ten minutes alone with her."

"You're bluffing!" Enraged, Frank pulled out his gun and aimed it at The Suit's head.

"Now, Frank, I don't think this is how either of us are going to get the answers we want, do you? And as you can see, I don't bluff."

The bodyguard appeared, noisily pushing Sarah through the tall grass toward them, leering. One beefy arm was solidly wrapped around her neck, the other under her shirt, groping her breast.

They told the orderly at the front desk who they were there to see. Her eyebrows raised in surprise, "No one's ever come to see her. Are you sure you have the right person?"

They assured her they did, signed in, then followed her up the dark stairwell to the room. The door was open, the woman sat in the sturdy hospital bed, overflowing it, her obese belly flopping over the railings, her unwashed hair matted and wild, bald in spots where it had been torn out.

Her hands were shackled with cloth ties to the bed. "To keep her from pulling any more out."

She smelled as bad as she looked. Ann pushed past the almost visible wall of her body odors, deeper into the room, up to her bedside. The aged woman spoke without opening her eyes, "Get the hell out of here."

Ann stepped backward in surprise. Tony was right there. "Um, I will. I just need a few minutes of your..."

"I SAID GET THE HELL OUT! ARE YOU DEAF, YOU LITTLE BITCH?"

Now Ann fled the room. The orderly was standing in the hallway, waiting. "We call her Little Miss Sunshine. I don't know what you want with her, but my advice would be to forget about it."

Tony held her close. "What do you want to do, babe?"

"It's not about what I want to do. It's what I have to do. I have to go back in there. I have to finish this."

She marched in bravely and spoke with authority, "You don't know who I am, but I know who you are, and you are going to sit there and listen until I'm done talking! Now open your eyes and look at me!"

"Fuck you! Here, is this what you want?" She opened her eyelids wide. Behind them were empty sockets and bright red tissue. It looked like her skull was packed with bloody raw hamburger, threatening to ooze out.

Ann recoiled, shocked. She ran past Tony and the orderly, downstairs and out the front door into the parking lot, hyperventilating.

The entire way and for the rest of her life, in her worst nightmares she heard the echoes of the Crazy Lady cackling loudly and saw yellow puss and blood running down her greasy cheeks from the holes where her eyeballs should have been.

⌒*ᵱ*⌒

"So let's do it this way. I ask a question, you answer. Then it's your turn. There's no reason for me to hide anything from you now, since you and I both know how this ends." Suit waved nonchalantly at the lake. "That was brilliant, you know, luring me here by making me think that someone else had discovered my little secret. But it's really just your pathetic little attempt at vengeance, isn't it?"

"Is that your first question?"

"Only if that's yours."

"What, your original forays into legitimate business ventures weren't enough, you had to bring that crazy woman partner in to be the softer, feminine side of your illegal schemes?"

"You have it all wrong, Frank. She came to me. She was the mastermind, I was just the funding and security for our venture. At least at first. It was never more than just business for me, but it was a personal vendetta for her. It took over. She began losing her edge when she began losing her sight. And when we were unable to tie up some loose ends, she became even more unstable. She became a deficit to me. I terminated her operations after her breakdown."

"Well, you should know others have discovered many of your little secrets as you call them, and we are going to enjoy watching you get exposed for the piece of lowlife scum you are. You can dress a piece of shit up in a fancy suit, douse it with the most expensive cologne money can buy, but at the end of the day, you'll always smell like ass."

"Clever. I am confident I have covered my tracks very well over the years, however. I am seen as an important businessman in this city. I've brought in the revenue, which has funded numerous building projects, technological advancements and civic growth."

"Which is why so many have turned a blind eye."

"It wasn't by their choice. I kept them in the dark, using my Overseas Franchise Administration connections to funnel resources in and out under assumed names. Useful products fronted my more lucrative investments."

"You mean the wholesale selling of babies on the black market."

"Oh, you make it sound so negative. The children of this nation may have once been considered its greatest natural resource, but you and I both know that time is long past. Just google the words 'baby sold' and you will get a partial list of the many creative ways even their own parents have increased the value of these otherwise unwanted children."

"But you took advantage of the most vulnerable in our society, feeding on the weakness of young mothers, even going so far as creating a false outreach to the poor and helpless, a false alternative in your One For All 'ministry.'"

"Ha, I did society a favor. Nobody else wants to deal with these losers—not families, not churches, not the government, not society. Nobody even noticed they were missing. And nobody cares about the tissue they produce.

As far as I see it, I added to their worth and value on this planet."

"You disposed of those women in a furnace! How can you possibly justify that?"

"I saved taxpayers thousands of dollars in welfare costs. I saved their families and society the added expense of these dependents and their offspring. Lest you get too holier than thou, you have also disposed of someone in the furnace. Isn't that where my head of security disappeared to? And here we thought he'd run off with Dickerson's money. I underestimated you, Frank."

"You pretended to reach out to women who were impregnated by rape. They didn't choose that!"

"Well, I supposed they could have had abortions, but I think that would have been such a waste of a delicious young life, don't you?" He grinned at Frank.

Disgusted, Frank lunged at The Suit and pushed the gun barrel into his temple. He spoke to the bodyguard, "It appears we are at a standoff. Let my wife go and I will let your boss go."

The giant shook his head and began to tighten his arm around Sarah's neck, pulling until her blood vessels popped out against her skin, her face turning blue, her body slumping against him helplessly. Uncertain, Frank turned the gun toward him. The Suit kicked him hard in the stomach and he doubled over in pain, dropping the heavy pistol. The Suit reached down to pick it up. A shot rang out. Then a second. Two bodies dropped.

"What do you mean you have to go back? I really don't think that's a good idea, Ann." Tony sat in the car with her, concern wrinkling his forehead.

"I haven't finished what I came to do. It's okay, Tony. I know this is what God wants me to do."

"Okay. I love you, Ann. You have my support. Let's go."

He opened the car door for her, reached in and grabbed the paper bag out of the backseat. "Don't want to forget this."

They walked in, up to the orderly at the front desk who shook her head incredulously. "Back for more, eh? You're not going to get anywhere with her, you know. She'd been this way ever since she got here five years ago. They'd found her in her apartment, a raving lunatic. She'd clawed out her own eyes. Crazy old lady."

"I just need a few minutes with her. Then I won't come back."

"Whatever you say, lady. I can give you ten minutes, but that's it. After you left yesterday she cried and screamed for hours. Kept hollering for her mama to bring her pills. Creeped me out. You really got to her. She's been mumbling nonsense ever since."

"We won't be long," Tony assured her.

They heard her before they got to her doorway. Her singsong voice repeated, "Blue pills, white pills, yellow, red. Listen to what mother said. Blue pills, white pills, yellow, red. Listen to what teacher said."

They walked in slowly, Ann unsure how to begin. She cleared her throat. "I just need a few minutes."

"No! No! No! You can't come here! You can't talk to me! No! No! No!"

"Shut up!" Ann surprised herself with the force of her words. "It's my turn to talk."

The woman froze. Ann began, "My name is Annabelle Laura. I was the baby you tried to dispose of twenty years ago because I was born without arms. I'm here to tell you I survived. Your driver, Dickerson, adopted me as a daughter, loved me and raised me. He taught me to love in return, to be kind, to forgive. I am here to tell you that though you tried to destroy me, God saved me. And I'm here to read you something."

"Kindness! Bah! That smelly bastard was kind to me and look where it got me—put in here! I've sat alone in darkness for the last five years. What could you possibly do to me? What you gonna do, thump me over the head with your Bible? I would welcome death at your hands. Ha! But you don't have any, do you! No hands! Ha ha! Broken, weak, worthless little bitch." She turned her head toward the far wall, dismissing and ignoring them. She began her singsong mantra again. "Blue, white, yellow, red...blue, white, yellow, red..."

~

Frank looked around in surprise. Sarah ran to him, as confused as he was until they saw him. Mr. Howsen appeared from a nearby hill, carrying a shotgun. "My wife always said I never was very good at minding my own business." They stared at him incredulously as he flipped open his phone to call the police.

⁓

Ann sat down next to the bed and nodded for Tony to pull out the book from the bag and place it on her lap. Ignoring the old woman's mindless ranting, she pulled open the cover and began to read. "The last thing Trish expected on her vacation in France was that she'd meet someone like Francisco. He was tall, had dark hair and wore a red beret. She'd scoffed at the idea of love at first sight until that fateful day on the sun scorched French beach." The old woman quieted, then visibly relaxed as Ann went on, the nightmare voices that had returned to taunt her for the past few years now drowned out by the fantasy world she entered through the words of the romance novel.

The orderly stopped by, surprised by what she saw in the room, and told Tony they could have all the time they needed. Ann read for hours.

It was to be the old woman's last reprieve. She died in her sleep early the next morning.

CHAPTER TEN

# The Answers

Tony's article for the religion section raised interest all over the city. He cited case after well-documented case of healings and deliverances through testimonials and copies of medical documents he obtained. Unequivocally, the churches that were experiencing these sorts of phenomena saw unprecedented growth. Not always in their Sunday service numbers, but in their community centers, small groups and outreaches. The data seemed to show that Jesus hadn't at all left the building, except to simultaneously work and act on behalf of the forgotten, the marginalized, the dubious. And His followers weren't far behind Him.

Howsen, Frank, Sarah and Ann returned to Scott's Pine, satisfied that OFA had lost its grip on the city. Ann and Tony continued their long-distance relationship through daily phone calls and the monthly trips he made to visit. She spent her days keeping the town clean and daydreaming about their next time together.

Reverend Phillips had his hands full providing oversight to the many things Sparta Baptist was involved in. Their fastest growth was in the Psalm 68 Project, which had developed out of the awareness he'd gained through the interviews he'd conducted throughout the city over the years. His eyes opened, he had naturally come into contact with young mothers in need. In fact, he began to see them everywhere he went, as if they were drawn to him.

He found people in both his church and others who were willing to become foster families to these girls. They took them in, gave them homes and emotional support. Nurses and doctors in these congregations donated their time and resources to give medical care. Counseling, tutoring and parenting classes were given, people sharing their vocations and giftings as they felt led to.

An adoption agency was developed with the concerns of mothers and babies paramount. Whenever it was possible and beneficial for both, open adoption was encouraged. Closed adoption was also a possibility when it was deemed appropriate. Each mother received post-adoption care and counseling no matter their decision. And most mothers stayed with or in contact with their own adoptive families in the church long after their crisis was over. They found healing through prayer, recovery groups, counseling and community. They found healing through the reassurance of their intrinsic value, their worth as beautiful women created by God—wanted, loved, seen, redeemed.

"Ann, I got a strange package at the office today. It's for you."

"For me? Why did they send it to the paper?"

"I'm not sure, but I think you should come here to open it."

"Wouldn't it be easier for you to send it to me?" she teased. "Or better yet bring it next weekend when you come visit?"

"About that. Something's come up. I won't be able to come after all. I really was hoping you'd be able to come here instead."

"Well, I'll see what Frank and Sarah have going on. Is everything okay, Tony?"

"Oh yes, just have some important things to take care of and can't get away right now. Let me know what you decide."

"I've already decided. I'm coming there even if I have to hitchhike. Although that'd be kind of difficult, you know, since I'd have to use my big toes as thumbs."

He laughed. "I'll talk to you soon then. I love you."

"I love you, too."

She hung up and went to the next door apartment. "Do we have plans for the weekend?"

"Yes, we do. It's jam packed!" Frank informed her.

"Oh, yes, I'd forgotten to tell you, dear. I hope Tony's not coming. It definitely won't be a good time for him to visit here."

Disappointed, Ann missed the teasing tone in their voices as they went on. "Yep, we really won't be here at all."

"Because we have that thing we're doing."

"And then there's the other thing, don't forget that!"

"Oh yes, I had. But it's okay. We can fit it in after the thing with the thing."

Ann was getting annoyed at their banter. "What are you talking about? What are we doing all weekend?"

"Oh, we didn't tell you? We're going to the city." Sarah smiled.

"We are? Why?"

"Reverend Phillips has asked us to be there for the ribbon-cutting of their new building construction. It will house the Psalm 68 Project, among other things."

Ann's tone was mock indignant, "How long have you known about this?"

"Oh, I've known about it for a long time, longer than my wife, that's for sure."

"No, I'm pretty sure I told you about it, so..."

"If I remember right, it was my idea." Frank smirked.

"Your memory must be slipping, dear. I hate to say it. I definitely have known about it much longer than you have."

Ann left them, happy that games were again being played in their home, happy about the success of the Psalm 68 Project, and happy at the prospect of seeing Tony again soon.

⌎⌎

They got into town just in time to rush to the church for the ceremony. Tony was there, he found Ann and hugged her quickly before they sat down on the folding chairs in the front row where Reverend Phillips had directed them. "Hello, beautiful!"

A pink ribbon stretched around the perimeter of the construction site where the new building would sit, next to the large, stately church. An enlarged mockup of it sat on an oversized easel. Reverend Phillips stepped up to the podium and spoke into a microphone.

"Thank you all for coming! We are privileged to be able to embark on this new adventure together, as a church, as a community, as a family. What God has opened up for us in the past few years is astounding! We've gone from a building full of half-asleep consumers of the gospel to full-fledged book of Acts followers of Jesus!" Applause and "amens" erupted in the crowd.

"Seeds of social justice have been planted on this land for over 200 years. God himself has seen fit to awaken and nourish them into fruit. We are again sustained by the roots of our calling, to love God, to love others. We are not the producers of it, but the gardeners only. And we gladly give it away."

When this next round of applause subsided, he turned to Ann. "With your permission, we would like to dedicate this building to the cause of freedom for all who are in bondage, any without hope, those without resources. And we would like to name it after you, Ann."

Overcome with emotion, she sat frozen. Everyone was on their feet around her, cheering and clapping loudly. Tony whispered close to her ear to be heard, "Darling, I think you are supposed to go up and make a speech now."

A glance at Frank and Sarah's proud faces told her they'd known all along. Tony walked her to the podium. He spoke into the mic, "I know you want to hear from this beautiful woman here, and I hate to argue with a man of the cloth, but I believe you've made a mistake, Reverend." Reverend Phillips smiled and nodded.

"You see, you weren't very specific in your speech. I believe what you failed to mention to Ann is that, with your permission," he looked at her now, "we want to christen this building the Annabelle Laura Burton Home." He waited until what he'd said sunk in.

She looked at him, searching his eyes, "Do you mean?"

"Yes, Ann. Will you marry me?"

He barely heard her say yes over the thunderous congratulations of the crowd.

"How do you know it's for me? It has your name on the box."

He fidgeted uncomfortably before admitting, "The note inside the envelope said, 'for the girl with no arms.'"

"Yep, that's pretty specific." Ann smiled. Then frowned when she saw the return address: Sandstone Sanitarium.

"See, here it is." He pulled the little handwritten note out of the top drawer of his desk. "It also says, 'Miss Sunshine wanted you to have this.'"

She shivered a little, swallowed the lump in her throat and asked him to open it. Inside was the paper bag they'd left behind. He turned it upside down and out fell a book.

It was a thick, hardcover romance novel. EXTRA LARGE PRINT emblazoned across the front, a steamy picture of a man and woman locked in embrace on the cover.

"I don't understand?"

"Me either. Maybe it was her favorite book or something?"

"Well, what would I possibly want with that evil woman's book? Just throw it away, Tony."

He went to push it into the trash can next to his desk but missed. It landed on the floor at Ann's feet.

"Holy crap!" he exclaimed as they both stood there, staring at it, unbelieving. The cover had flopped open and carved into the pages of the book itself was a hidden compartment, big enough for a small journal to fit inside. When he pulled it out he immediately recognized the name of the woman who'd written her name in scrawling letters on the first page. They had just found Jane Sentmore, the nurse from the second missing person's report, through the pages of this, her diary.

It outlined in detail the comings and goings of OFA. They sat there in Tony's office, reading the accounts of a woman's descent into darkness. They started by reading about the first day she'd signed on with this *"promising company who are going to pay me more than I could ever make in mainstream medicine."* Then they skipped to her last entry. *"I hope what I did for Frank Longly helped. I hope I have finally done something right, something good."*

They read her detailed accounts of the year she'd worked for OFA. Tony tried to skip over the part about Ann's birth, but she insisted he read it. He choked out the words through tears:

> *Today's delivery was different. She wasn't the usual basket case crack head they usually find. She said she was going to escape the warehouse with the baby and give her a good life. After the baby was born she wanted to hold her. Boss lady had her nose stuck in one of her stupid books. What could it hurt, right? She held her like she didn't even notice anything wrong with those nubby little arms. She told her not to worry, that God would watch over her all the days of her life. That she was really something special. The sedative kicked in. I wrapped the baby up, pulled the sheet over the mom's head and did what I've done a hundred times over the past year. I handed a baby to a monster and stuck a syringe into a mother. No matter how they label it "mercy killing, damage control, just business." How could I possibly do it one more time? How could I? I tried to tell boss lady about her disability but the greedy bitch just wanted to get her hands on the filthy money. She got all huffy with me and drove away, the baby wrapped in an old blanket and stuffed into her disgusting carpet bag. I bet that was one pissed off businessman when they tried to pawn off damaged goods! They brought me down to corporate that night*

*and asked me to finish things off. I pushed just enough of the syringe into her little body to slow her vital functions. They thought she was dead. I bet Dickerson got quite a shock a few hours later!*

Tony looked at her. "That's it."

They sat in silence for a while, at a loss for words.

"You have to print it, Tony. All of it. It's a really big story."

"No, I don't. I can just put it in the trash, Ann. Nobody needs to know all these things about you. I told Sarah when I first met her that I would never hurt you. And I meant it."

"Tony, this is all part of my story, but it doesn't define me. I am making my own story now, with you, our story. The truth is my mother wanted me." She choked on these words. Sobs subsiding, she went on, "This is her story, too. And it honors her. It honors all those who have been humiliated and dehumanized by OFA, the sex trade, and it calls to action those who've turned a blind eye. Every entry you publish removes the lie of this being "just business" or "just the way the world is" and draws attention to the fact that these are people, human beings. Not commodities. And it is time for all of us to pull our heads out of the sand and act on their behalf."

"Okay, I'll start writing it now. I love you, Ann."

"I love you, Tony. I'll help you. We'll do it together."

And they did.

His article was reprinted in every newspaper in the country. Millions of readers were shocked and outraged that such things were happening in America. Public outcry demanded swift government action. The city took hold of all OFA assets and demolished the warehouse. Voters called for immediate measures to be put in place for the protection of the children. Facebook was livid with clever memes and shared blogs calling for stricter penalties and punishment for perpetrators. The talk around the nation's collective water coolers was the sordid details of OFA and the passionate admonition that "something has to be done." This lasted for about two weeks. Then March Madness began.

# The New Birth

She rode the ups and downs of this, her first labor and delivery, like a long-awaited roller coaster. Her husband stood beside her, wiping away the sweat pouring down her face. She smiled at him between contractions, grateful for his encouragement and calming presence.

They'd been here at the hospital for twelve hours. She was tired but anxious to meet the little person who'd been nesting inside her for the nine months since her honeymoon. She chuckled at the teasing they'd gotten from friends and family.

Suddenly she knew it was time to bear down, had no choice really. The doctor and nurse confirmed it, "Push, dear." She did. With all the pent up love of an expectant mother, the strength of a survivor, the will of a beloved daughter and the desire of a wife in love, she pushed.

Past the pressure of a head and agony of shoulders she felt the release of the child expelled from her body. She began weeping, relieved and delighted even before she heard the baby's first cry. She closed her eyes and let the emotions wash over her, thoroughly overwhelmed.

"Annabelle? Hey, honey. Do you want to hold our baby?" she heard Tony's scratchy voice working through the lump in his throat.

She opened her eyes and sat up, then, searching for their child. The nurse placed the swaddled bundle onto her chest, smiling. "Congratulations, Ann!"

Ann enjoyed the warmth and smell for a few minutes. She folded her arms around the baby and a shadow crossed her face as she saw them. Her nubs lay calloused, coarse and ugly against the infant's soft blanket.

Tony reached over and gave them a loving squeeze. "I'd like to show you something, honey." Fearfully she watched him as he picked up the baby and began stripping off the coverings on the little body. "I asked the nurse to let me show you myself."

Her eyes were glued to the newborn, searching hopefully as her husband unwrapped their little present. "Here he is, Ann."

"He? We have a boy?"

"Yes, my love."

"And he's got...you know?"

"Yes, he's got both you-knows."

He put the naked little body on her chest and pulled a blanket over the both of them. She wept softly, overcome with relief and joy. She held his flawless little body close. "We'll call him Thomas."

Tony agreed. "Yes. Thomas is the perfect name for our

beautiful little boy."

⸻

"Are you ready to go to the hospital to see Ann?" she asked as she entered the shop. He'd been working out here all morning.

"Hi, babe. I'm almost done. I just want to finish this one thing."

Sarah walked to the worktable and looked on, admiring his work. He'd outdone himself with this latest project. He'd spent countless hours on it, working late into the night and rising early for weeks. The intricacies he'd put into the wood were testament to the diligent, careful hand of an artist and craftsman. She'd had no idea he could do such beautiful woodwork. Neither had he.

He had been drawn to this. The idea had been fully formed in his head one morning when he woke up. He'd bought the most beautiful, solid block of wood he could find and some carving tools. Then he's sat dumbly in front of it with no idea how to begin. He'd never done anything like this before. He'd done construction, maintenance, rebuilt engines, but this would take fine motor precision and experience. He had neither.

But he saw it complete in his mind's eye and he knew he was called to do it. So he picked up a pencil and began drawing on the face of this unfamiliar, unlikely canvas.

That was months ago. Now it was finished, all but the last layer of protective coating, which he slathered generously over it now. It had to last, had to withstand the weather. He brushed his gratitude and awe over this labor of love. Finished, he turned to Sarah, tears running down his face. He pulled her close and whispered, "It's done."

"Frank, it's beautiful! She'll love it."

They left to go meet their new grandson.

～✲～

Three days later they brought the new mommy and baby Thomas home. As they were walking into the house Ann suddenly stopped, concerned. "Wait, there's something wrong."

"What do you mean?" Tony asked, glancing at Frank.

"In the backyard, something's different!"

Frank spoke up, "Maybe you should go check it out, Annabelle."

She caught their smiling faces. Confused, she slowly walked to the tree her father's body rested under. His gravesite had clearly been disturbed. The cross Sarah had made was still there, but it had been placed inside a large, intricately carved headstone. It was one of the most beautiful things she'd ever seen.

Their story had been carved into the wood. There were jazz saxophones and trumpets with music notes, pictures of bears standing on two feet, arms upraised, whose faces looked suspiciously like her father's, stacks of books piled up and toppling over into opened pages with nursery rhymes and classics etched on their spines. There were even cars flying through the open sky, with her father in a super hero cape, a laughing baby, or a smiling cat at the wheel. Ann laughed at the various poses of the cats that filled every spare inch of the space, like her father had pretended they did in real life. Delighted and touched, she laughed and laughed. It was perfect.

Across the top in ornate capital letters she traced the letters slowly with her eyes. They spelled out T-H-O-M-A-S D-I-C-K-E-R-S-O-N.

She felt them all then. The family she'd been given were all standing with her. Tony held little Thomas with one arm and wrapped his other around her. Frank and Sarah stood quietly behind her, holding hands. They all looked on at the memorial of the man who'd given them this moment together, remembering gratefully.

"Thank you," she whispered. To her father, to all of them, to God himself, "Thank you."

## THE BEGINNING

## TARA

She had awakened in an alley fifteen years ago and wasn't sure how she'd gotten there. She vaguely remembered a hospital room, a smiling nurse in white, a baby.

A young man in a large cowboy hat had walked by her, "Lady, are you okay?" She looked down at her legs, rolled in a white sheet, blood spreading across her pelvis and thighs.

"No, I don't guess I am." He'd called an ambulance for her and she'd recovered over the next few weeks.

"Ma'am, you had high levels of an unknown toxin in your blood stream. We believe that has damaged your CNS, making it impossible for you to walk again." The doctor lingered, clearly uncomfortable.

"Is there more, doctor?"

"Yes. You recently gave birth, but we have no records of the baby. And I regret to inform you that you have sustained damage to the point where you will not be able to have children in the future. I'm sorry." He looked sincere.

The police came to question her. Convinced she had no idea what had happened to her or her baby, they let her go.

She spent most of her time living under the bridge with her friends. Many were people like her—out of touch with their past, lacking plans for the future—and lonely. Some, like her, lived with a haunting desire to find their something special. Some of their ghosts had names. Hers was nameless, yet her arms ached for the baby nonetheless.

She was startled early one Sunday morning. "What?!" She looked around, searching for the voice that had awakened her. No one was there. She closed her tired eyes, hoping to fall back asleep for another hour or so. She heard it again. "Sparta Baptist." She woke up her buddy and he helped her get out of her sleeping bag and into her chair.

"Where you goin?"

"I'm going to church. You want to come with?" she asked him.

"No, I gotta go find my wife."

"Suit yourself, Frank." She wheeled herself to the church and parked her chair in back. It was a pretty normal church service until the offering.